WILDE SHORTS

A FOREVER WILDE COLLECTION

LUCY LENNOX

Cover Art: Beth Cranford
Editing: One Love Editing

BLURB

Wilde Shorts is a collection of Happy Ever Afters featuring princes, valets, professors, and even a snarky, raccoon-stealing fan-favorite. Grab this collection to read the following stories:

Princeling: royal flash fiction featuring the beloved characters from *Felix and the Prince.*

The Billionaire's Valet: a short-story featuring King Lior's childhood best friend, Iggy, who races across Africa with a broken heart in search of the dedicated valet who's always loved him.

Flirt: a laugh-out-loud novella featuring snarky Stevie and the grumpy fire chief who can't stay away from him. Cameos include one unexpected raccoon named Zorro.

Arthur & Max: the story that comes after the epilogue of *Wilde Love,* featuring King Lior's valet and a super-sweet Wilde cousin who's always wanted his very own Wilde love.

Professor Platonic: a student/professor story featuring a Wilde cousin and his greatest enemy. When Jack Wilde loses out on an incredible research opportunity, he goes looking for platonic comfort to distract him from taking wild revenge on the professor who screwed him over. Only... the man who shows up to offer comfort is none other than the professor who caused the problem in the first place.

All of the stories included in Wilde Shorts are set in the Forever Wilde world. With the exception of Princeling, all of them can be enjoyed on their own without reading other books in the Forever Wilde series.

PRINCELING

1

FELIX

I STARED down at the tiny little human raisin. He was so frail and beautiful. I couldn't stop staring.

"It's too much," I murmured. "The weight of a name like that will tip the poor kid over."

Hen scoffed. "Oh please. He can handle it. He's a Wilde."

Lio snapped his head around and glared at his sister. "I beg your pardon. He's the heir to the Grimaldi throne."

She shrugged. "He's half-Grimaldi and half-Wilde. Here's hoping the Wilde part dominates."

Lio glanced at me and his entire expression softened. "You have a point. That wouldn't be so bad, would it?"

My heart did it's usual *ka-thunk* when Lio looked at me like that. Like I was the sun and he lived to bask in my warmth. It never got old.

"Can we at least not call him Harald? Ever?"

I looked back down at our son, the product of my cousin Winnie's egg and Lio's sperm, incubated for the past nine months inside of the healthy womb of one of Lio and Hen's distant cousins. Sophie had given us the most amazing gift ever. She'd taken such good care of him, stayed healthy throughout the pregnancy, and had invited us to every single appointment with her.

I looked over at where she lay sprawled on the giant bed in her suite in the castle. She'd insisted on nursing him for at least the first couple of weeks even though her own two kids were at home begging for their mother to return from "making Uncle Felix and Lior's baby."

"All I have to do is flip a boob out from time-to-time and let the royal servants wait on me hand and food for two weeks? Sign me up," she'd said with a sigh, sinking into the luxurious feather bed.

She currently slurped some kind of fruit smoothie she'd instructed the kitchen to make for her. The "I gave birth to the future king and all I got was this lousy T-shirt" shirt she wore stretched across her giant boobs. I was desperate to take a Sharpie to the shirt and add "and a summer home on the Riviera" to the bottom of the shirt, but Lio suggested that would be in poor taste.

"No Harald," Lio agreed. "But it has to stay in the name for reasons. Howabout calling him Chris? That's very American-sounding."

I looked down at his tiny face. Christien Triannon Felix William Weston Harald Grimaldi of Liorland stared back at me with his star-tlingly blue eyes. "I can't stand it," I whispered. "How is it possible to love someone this much?"

Lio's voice was as reverent as I felt. "It's easy."

I glanced up at him, but instead of looking at the baby, he was gazing at me again.

How was this my life? It just kept getting better and better.

~

Flash Fiction prompt suggested by Lair members Sheena J Himes and Sarah Townsend, among many others!

THE BILLIONAIRE'S VALET

1

IGGY

"Where the fuck are you?" Lio asked. Even though I was almost 9,000 miles away from my best friend, he sounded just as loudly annoyed as if he were standing next to my ear.

"Cape Town, South Africa," I admitted, feeling a little sheepish. To be fair, when most people got bad news, they drowned their sorrows at the local pub, drinking two—or twelve—too many pints.

When I got bad news—the worst news—I apparently made spontaneous safari adventure plans.

I sighed. "Don't start."

"I already started," he snapped. "Everyone's worried sick. Your father said you've barely spoken a word since you heard."

I raked shaky fingers through my hair for the millionth time. No doubt I looked half-crazed, which was perhaps a good thing. My expensive clothes and Tumi carry-on made me a sitting duck in the crowd of travelers trying to find ground transportation.

Normally, I would have only needed to look for my name on a tasteful sign indicating the car and driver that my valet—who was also my bodyguard, secretary, confidant, and the gravity that kept my personal solar system aligned—had arranged for me. But nothing was normal about this trip, considering I'd booked it myself while drunk and sobbing on the marble floor of my foyer.

"What news?" I asked, feigning casual disinterest. "My valet quit. Big deal."

Lio made a choking, sputtering noise. "Jon Banks has been with you since we were fourteen years old. He's your best fucking friend."

"*You're* my best fucking friend," I corrected, trying to ignore the fierce jab to my heart at hearing Jon's name spoken out loud. "B-banks was an employee, nothing more."

"Bullshit. I know you're hurting. Did he explain? Give you a reason? Anything? I asked Arthur, and he said Banks has kept everything close to the vest."

My lips felt numb as I thought about Jon's fierce loyalty. Of course he wouldn't have said anything to Lio's valet. I could have shot Banks in the kneecap for a lark, and he would have told the authorities he tripped and fell onto a bullet. I could just hear his soft, familiar murmur. *"Silly me."*

I swallowed around a lump in my throat and wondered if I'd reached humiliation's rock bottom yet. If I had one shred of dignity left, I'd fling it merrily by the wayside with another desperate text or call to Jon's number, but I wasn't strong enough to wait for another response that wasn't coming. Instead, I kept Lio on the phone as long as I could to keep myself from breaking my own damned heart.

"How's Felix?" I asked, feigning a cheery grin. "Still worshipping the porcelain gods?"

Lio let out a fond sigh. "I keep trying to tell my husband, sympathy morning sickness isn't a thing. Our poor surrogate though. She's having a rough time of it."

My best friend, the king of Liorland, the man I'd slept with a thousand times to help scratch my own itch and allow him to do the same while keeping his sexuality out of the tabloids, had finally found love. It had meant an end to our casual friends-with-benefits scheme and the beginning of a giant, excruciating, mostly dry spell for me.

"I'm sorry," I said. "Pregnancy's hard enough without being watched by the entire world."

"Yeah. Everyone has a fucking opinion—like it's any of their damned business. But she's hanging in there. She's strong as hell."

I let out a relieved breath. Talking about Lio and Felix's pregnancy journey was a safe topic. They already had a son named Chris, who was the light of all our lives. Part of me hoped the next one was a fiery little girl who gave them a run for their money.

"Boy or girl, you have to promise to put Ignatius somewhere in her name. You royals like lots of names, so no one will ever notice."

He scoffed. "You think I don't notice you trying to change the subject, but I do. I know you're hurting. And I know you're hiding."

"I've loved him half my life," I whispered, the words so small I could barely hear them myself.

"I know." Lio's voice was affectionate and kind. "And you need to tell him."

I barked out a laugh, enough for three women near me in baggage claim to edge farther away. "Been there, done that. Have the rejection memories—many of them, by the way—to prove it."

Lio hadn't always known about my crush on Jon. But then I'd lost control one night and blabbed to Felix, who'd gone straight to Lio to discuss "what we should do about Ignatius."

"Iggy... confessing your crush to Banks as a young teenager doesn't count. He was ten years older than your skinny ass and would have been arrested on the spot for even considering it. Confessing again in a blackout-drunken stupor on your eighteenth birthday was also a poor choice. Besides the fact your parents were in the next room for our Hotchkiss graduation, Banks had also just returned from his mother's funeral in Arizona. After losing her, he couldn't afford to lose his job, too. You're a billionaire. He's your servant."

"Don't call him that."

Lio grunted. "Sorry."

"I was so fucking selfish," I said, rubbing my hand over my face. "What he must have thought of me."

I didn't correct Lio's assessment of how drunk I was. It was easier to let him think I could hardly remember that night than to admit I remembered it all: The desperate plea in my voice. The calm look of tender pity in Jon's eyes. The feel of his hands on my body as he carefully unbuttoned my shirt only moments before racing me into the bathroom to vomit.

My face flushed with embarrassment as though it had happened last night instead of years ago.

"You've never given up on anything in your life," Lio insisted. "Banks loves you. Find him. Talk to him."

I knew Jon loved me. He loved me like one loves an errant but earnest child. Like one loves a longtime coworker with whom they've shared hundreds of inside jokes. Like one loves a benevolent employer.

Meaning: not anywhere close to the kind of love I wanted from Jonathan Banks.

"I've tried. He won't answer my calls." The lump in my throat grew to threatening proportions. "He didn't even say goodbye. Just thanked my father for his years of employment and said it was time to pursue a new dream. Time to move on."

"Really?" Lio asked, sounding suddenly perky. "He said it like that?"

Across the baggage hall, an older man in a dark suit held a sign with my destination on it. I began walking in his direction.

"That's what Dad said. But I'm not sure what it could possibly mean. Jon's dream has always been a simple one: To have his own vegetable-and-flower garden. A dog. Peace and quiet. That's it... that's the dream. I've told him a million times we could move anywhere in the world to make that a reality. I can work from anywhere. I just wanted him to be happy."

"He'd never ask you to go out of your way for him."

"Or maybe his dream just didn't include me," I said lightly, like acknowledging that truth didn't rip my heart from my chest. I took a deep breath and made eye contact with my driver, giving him a slight nod to indicate he had the right passenger.

"Could he have had a different dream? Something you didn't know about?"

If he'd asked me two days ago, I would have assured him there was nothing I didn't know about Jon. His fondness for schedules and dislike of movie remakes. The growl in his voice when I teased him for either. The precise scent of my pomade when he applied it to my hair, which was so much different and better than when I applied it myself.

But now Jon was gone, and I wasn't sure of much anymore.

I handed my rolling suitcase off to the driver. "There was one other thing he mentioned a long time ago."

"What was it?" Lio asked.

"He always wanted to take the Blue Train through South Africa. He wanted to go on safari."

2

———————

JON

I STEPPED onto the platform and took in the long line of sleek blue train carriages with a clean white stripe down the sides. Being here was bittersweet. On the one hand, I'd never expected to actually make it to my dream holiday. On the other, I'd only pulled the trigger on such an extravagant expense to get me as far away as possible from the man I loved.

After all these years, I never expected the final straw would be something as benign as a fancy-dress fundraiser, but it was.

As I'd helped him with his costume that night—a simple white tank top and baseball cap wig—Iggy had vibrated with excitement. He'd chosen it to create a stir, and as usual, once Iggy fixed his heart on something, nothing on earth would shake him. He'd considered that night's costume his "funniest, sexiest" idea to date.

But as I stepped close to apply the large "No Ragrets" tattoo to Iggy's waxed upper chest and prepared to watch him walk out the door without me once again, I began to feel the deep, soul-crushing irony of the tattoo's message.

Had I stepped forward another few inches, the tip of my nose would have fit perfectly into the dip between his collarbone, smelling his Jo Malone Whisky & Cedarwood cologne and feeling the warm comfort of his skin against mine. I'd imagined it so often in recent years that it felt familiar. *Right*. Even though it was impossible.

When I'd come to work for the Corbridge family, I'd never imagined feeling this way. Back then, my charge had been a teen boy who was more legs than sense and had a mouth ten times bigger than he was. I'd felt more like a babysitter than a valet—a six-year veteran of the British Army, tasked to keep the chancellor of the exchequer's son from getting into trouble.

Thanks to meeting an actual royal valet while there, the indomitable Arthur, I'd done my job well. Eight years later, I'd brought Iggy home safely with an Ivy League college degree as well.

I'd assumed Iggy would let me go then, no matter how fond we'd grown of each other, but I'd been pleasantly surprised.

He'd made me his valet and social secretary, entrusting me with everything related to his personal life—his house, his wardrobe, and his calendar. Moreover, he'd made me his *friend*, sharing with me a decade's worth of dreams and aspirations, endless sexual conquests and near-misses, and all the failures and triumphs of the work he'd chosen to do.

Ignatius Corbridge was passionate about being out. He was loud and proud about his bisexuality and did his best to make sure others could do the same by lobbying European governments and advocating for global victims of hate crimes. With his high-level political connections, Iggy had become a force to be reckoned with.

In short order, the rebellious teenager I'd been fond of had become a determined, witty, kind, joyful man I needed like oxygen. I'd fallen deeply in love with him, despite our age difference. Despite being his employee. And I'd treasured every moment in his company so damn much that I'd thought, *This is enough, Jon. If you only get to love him this way, you can be satisfied.*

Which only made it harder to witness what happened next.

I couldn't point to the time when his partying lifestyle began changing from simple good fun to something more. Maybe a few years ago, when his friend Lio had fallen in love with an American and shocked the world by coming out and marrying him. Perhaps more recently. But suddenly, the brilliant man who could do or be anything he chose had... changed.

Iggy no longer spent time with people like Felix and Lio who loved him, or with his sister and nieces and nephews, whom he adored; but with a crowd of hangers-on who only valued his name and status. He'd stopped encouraging me to attend events with him —invitations I'd always appreciated, though never accepted.

He didn't talk to me about the parties he attended or the people he'd met, let alone the people he went home with on a near-nightly basis.

In fact, he hardly spoke to me anymore at all.

On the rare occasions he was home, there was a kind of restless energy to him, like he couldn't wait to be away again.

It was clear that whatever place I'd had in his life was no longer mine. I couldn't stop it, and I'd known, as certainly as I knew I loved him, that I couldn't stand by and watch distance grow between us.

So I'd smoothed the tattoo over his chest, taking way too much time to press it against his hot skin. I'd waited for him to walk out the door. Then I'd packed my things and left.

For four straight days, I'd had to practically handcuff myself to the hotel bed to keep from flinging myself at his feet in apology and begging to come home.

I'd never wanted anything more than I wanted Ignatius Corbridge, but he wasn't meant for me. There were a million reasons why—the twenty years of personal service between us, the fact that I was a former soldier with no degrees and no pedigree, while he was an elite member of the posh set, born with a silver-and-diamond chandelier shining down on him from above. But the most important was that Iggy was going places, and I was so very bone-tired of watching him go without me.

It was high time I went somewhere myself.

The train platform was busy, but not nearly as crowded as a commuter platform would be. This luxury liner carried fewer than a hundred passengers, which was good. I was in South Africa searching for peace and quiet.

The beginning of a new life, I thought as I stepped into the car. *My fresh start.*

Working for the Corbridge family had been lucrative. It was one of the reasons I stayed for so long, even when it started to break me. Taking a safari train through Africa was a dream come true, and I wouldn't have been able to afford it without Iggy and his family. I was grateful, truly.

Now, I would use this journey to plan my future—a cozy life in a small, picturesque village somewhere outside of London where I could afford a cottage with a garden. A life where I wasn't Iggy's valet or Iggy's friend or Iggy's... anything. I would simply be—

"Jon!"

I closed my eyes and told myself I was imagining the familiar voice. I refused to waste this trip with a detour to a mental facility.

I opened my eyes and took another step, and then I heard it again.

"Jonathan Banks."

I turned around slowly to see both the best and worst thing that could possibly be following me onto this train.

Ignatius Corbridge.

The absolute, without-a-doubt, hands-down love of my life.

3

———————

IGGY

SETTING eyes on Jon's primly styled dark hair and his trim figure made me nearly stumble into the porter passing me with a luggage trolly.

Unlike my own hot-mess self, Jon was dressed impeccably in slim-fit trousers and a pristine button-down. His polished brown leather shoes looked right at home on the burgundy-and-gold carpeting of the luxury train car.

I called out his name in shock, unable to believe he was really here. The Jonathan Banks I knew would never actually splurge on his dream holiday. He would have reasoned himself down to a budget-minded mini-break at the West Midland Safari Park back home.

But when I saw him hesitate at the sound of my voice, I knew it was truly him. Jon had spent twenty years responding to my voice, and it was most likely ingrained in him by now.

Which was why it felt so strange to watch him blatantly ignore it.

"Jonathan Banks," I called, suddenly annoyed at being ignored.

This time, he turned. The hesitation was clear in the coiled muscles of his back. "No," he said simply before continuing down the narrow hallway of the carriage.

I stared after him. '*No?*' What the fuck was that supposed to mean?

"This way, Mr. Corbridge. Your suite is the second door on the left just here." The porter seemed not to have caught the tension in the air between me and a fellow passenger, but I had. It had filled my lungs with sludge and threatened to choke me.

I followed the man without thinking, entering my private suite and nodding along as he pointed things out. My brain was too busy shuffling through possible reasons for Banks's snub to pay attention.

Had he quit because he didn't like me anymore? Or...

An idea blasted through my mind like a rogue firework shot sideways and racing straight for a crowd of people.

Was he sick? Was he dying? Had he quit his job and indulged in this once-in-a-lifetime trip because of some terrible, life-ending news?

I dragged in a breath. I needed to know if he was okay.

I thanked the butler, watched him leave, and immediately snuck out of the suite, creeping down the hallway like a criminal to the compartment I'd seen Jon enter.

I didn't knock or even warn him; I simply opened the door... and found him staring out the window with his hands in his pockets.

There was nothing to see other than the dirty white side of another train.

"Jon..." I began hesitantly. I'd never been a hesitant person. Once I established what I wanted, I made it happen. But there had also never been a time in my life, before now, that I'd doubted Banks or wondered how he'd receive me. "Are you okay?"

He didn't turn around, simply lowered his chin to his chest and sighed. "Why are you here, Iggy?"

"I..." How could I possibly answer his question without telling him of my desperation? Of the bone-chilling emptiness he'd left in his wake and my desire to do something, *anything*, to make me feel close to him again?

He shook his head and turned. His eyes roamed over me as if

assessing how I looked, how I felt, whether or not I was fit enough to be let loose in the world.

It had been his job, after all. And old habits surely died hard.

"You followed me," he accused. "On my own time. You..."

"No!" I said, too loudly. "I didn't know you would be here. I swear. I came because I...because..." I rubbed my face with both hands before firming my jaw. "I missed you." My voice broke a little. "And I can't... I don't... I..." Why was this so fucking hard? "I want to be with you."

There. I'd said it. The words I'd needed to say to him, exactly as Lio had instructed. Now we could move forward. Banks would understand my feelings. He always had.

Instead, he laughed without humor.

"You don't miss me. You miss having someone to clean up your messes. You miss having your life organized and handed to you on a platter, ready to eat. It's not me you miss, I promise."

His words reached into my chest and shredded my heart. How could he think so little of me? Of what we shared?

"You're wrong," I said, feeling anger well up like blood from a deep gash. "You have to know—"

"Go away, Iggy," he said, suddenly sounding exhausted. "I came here for peace. For escape. You're the opposite of that. It's why I left."

How long could a man stand in one place and continue to take armor-piercing rounds to the heart and gut?

"Can we talk about it?" I whispered.

He shook his head. I could see his jaw shift like he was clenching his teeth. Was this worse than I thought? Was it more than disinterest? Could it be... hate?

I nodded slowly and threw up a grin. I didn't care. None of this mattered. *See me here not caring. I will never care. I am the king of not taking things seriously.*

"Yeah, good. I understand. No problem. Enjoy your... trip." I gave him a jaunty salute like an absolute nutter and returned to my suite, where I could sit and stare into the side of the same dirty white train car.

Sometime later, the dirty white train began to move. It took me long minutes before I realized it was actually our train moving out of the station, not the other one.

It didn't matter. I would simply stay here and feel sorry for myself in this tiny train suite until we arrived in Pretoria in two days. Then I would fly back home to London. To my work. To my social obligations. To the days and nights stretched long and lonely ahead of me...

Utterly Jon-less and gray.

The sulk lasted several hours. I missed the special high tea to celebrate our departure, but I couldn't have cared less. It wasn't until the butler arrived to inform me about the formal dinner service that I realized I would need to actually eat if I wanted to have enough energy to continue my righteous indignation.

Besides, I'd moved from self-pity to anger strongly enough to change my mind about staying out of Jon's way. Why should I? I had as much right to enjoy my safari train vacation as the next arsehole.

I rallied by hopping in the tiny shower and banging my elbows and knees through a thorough wash before getting dressed in my trousers and shirt.

As soon as I realized what kind of shirt I'd packed, I nearly declared defeat.

French cuffs.

The kind that required cufflinks, eight hands, and a superhero level of patience I didn't have.

The kind that required... Jon.

4

JON

I COULDN'T DECIDE if Iggy was trying to make a point to annoy me or if it simply came naturally for him.

The banging and knocking between our suites were becoming comical. The man was over six feet of slim, strong muscle, so I had no trouble picturing him in the cramped quarters of a train car lavatory. But when I heard him bark out one of his favorite curse words and knock something over, I had to roll my eyes at the dramatics.

"Not my problem anymore," I murmured to myself.

"Sorry, sir?" the butler asked from the half-open doorway to my suite where he'd come to offer me assistance dressing.

The irony of this wasn't lost on me. I was getting a taste of Iggy's life.

I hadn't expected it to be so heartbreakingly lonely.

"Nothing. I was simply noticing my neighbor was awfully frustrated about something. It seems not everyone can relax on holiday."

He gave me a polite nod, but I could see the tiny curl of a smile. "Between you and me, sir, I believe he's attempting cufflinks for the first time. I told him I'd be in directly once I help you."

I stifled a laugh. There was no way Iggy would let a stranger touch him. Not only was his pride way too great to accept help under the best of conditions, but he'd also experienced an attempted kidnapping at age ten that had given him an aversion to being touched or cornered by people he didn't know.

There had been many times he'd called me in tears to come rescue him from uncomfortable situations. Thankfully, his aversion to touch had never included me.

"Good luck with that," I murmured with a smile.

But as the butler left, my gut began to churn with guilt. If Iggy needed help and he wouldn't accept it from the butler assigned to our carriage, maybe I...

No. I no longer worked for him. It wasn't my job to help him with cufflinks.

But as a friend...

I bit my lip. I needed to remember that Ignatius Corbridge and I weren't really friends. We'd been employer and employee for years. Yes, we'd been close. Intimate, even. But he'd pulled away. Shut me out. It wasn't my place to offer to help him with—

"Oh, for fuck's sake, it's just cufflinks," I spat into my empty suite. I moved quickly down the hall to Iggy's open door just as the butler escaped with an apology.

We exchanged awkward, polite smiles before I slipped inside.

"I said no, thank you," Iggy said between clenched teeth, looking down at his mangled cuffs.

"Alright then," I said primly, turning to leave. "I guess you don't need my help."

"Wait!" I heard a footstep before he stopped himself from coming after me. "Jon. Wait. Please... would you mind? You know how I am with these blasted things."

I moved closer and reached out a hand for the sterling silver cufflinks. When I saw they were my favorite pair, intricately detailed octopi with a tentacle for a stud, memory assaulted me.

"No mortal can do his own cufflinks, Jon. He'd need eight arms like this little creature. See?"

"Or he'd need to start buying button cuffs," I'd said practically, grateful for the excuse to hold his thick wrist in my hands and praying he never made that choice.

"Or they could get a Banks. It's the reason I keep you around, you know." His affectionate smile had told a different tale. "Sadly for them, I've got the only one."

I swallowed hard and reminded myself that had been *before*.

"Poor choice for traveling alone," I murmured.

"Mmph."

I concentrated on attaching the cuff while trying not to take a creepy, desperate inhale of his scent. While trying to ignore the warmth radiating off a body that had always run a full degree warmer than others. While trying not to meet his honey-flecked eyes.

It was nearly impossible. Keeping my calm with the man I wanted most in the world this close was going to break me.

"Why did you leave me?" Iggy's question was laid carefully into the air between us as if too delicate to be flung in my direction.

I took a deep, painful breath.

I'd known I'd have to explain myself if he ever happened to find me. Had prepared a polite answer to just this question. But the *me* on the end—not just why did I leave, but why did I leave *him*—hit my heart like a shrapnel bomb, and too many truths swamped me to force the lie out of my mouth.

Because I want to run my hands up your chest to your neck and cheeks and hair. I want to feel for once what it would be like to touch you as a lover instead of as a valet. I don't merely want to run your home; I want to be your home.

My fingers fumbled the cufflink, but Iggy caught it in the air, saving me from the degradation—and temptation—of getting on my knees at his feet to retrieve it.

While I secured the cufflink, I tried to ignore his long, strong fingers, the healthy veins under his tanned skin, the worn-out, faded cotton of a friendship bracelet that a child had made him at an outreach event. I had no doubt the boxer briefs he wore under his dark suit trousers were bright, brain-melting colors or novelty prints meant to give a laugh to anyone lucky enough to see them.

No matter how formal Ignatius Kirkwood Corbridge appeared, he remained the same caring, fun-loving Iggy underneath his clothes, and that reminder would be my undoing.

I ground my teeth and forced myself to remember how many people must have seen his underwear in recent years. He had very few limits when it came to who he slept with. Men, women, groups of both... it didn't matter.

To him.

It mattered to me though. Very much. And that was one of a thousand reasons why leaving was the right choice.

"There you are," I said, flashing him the same fake grin he'd pulled on me earlier. "Right as rain."

"Answer me," he demanded through his teeth. "Can't you just answer me?"

"You don't need me anymore."

"You're wrong," he gritted out. "So incredibly, mind-fuckingly wrong."

"Surely you can learn to dress yourself. Button cuffs are a simple solution."

He yanked his arm away, and I knew he was remembering the same conversation I had. "It's not about the cuffs, damn it. I don't need a valet, Jon. I need *you*. It's always been you. Don't you know that?"

Iggy searched my eyes. God only knew what he was looking for because I didn't.

"You're the only thing that made it bearable," he said softly.

His words slithered into my ears and took root like an unwelcome parasite. The parasite lied. But it was a seductive liar, one whose sibilant come-ons could very easily lead me down a dangerous path.

I saw a video once, of a machine whose sole job was to crush cars in a skip yard. I felt like my heart had somehow found its way into one and was being squeezed into nothing.

He didn't mean this... any of it. Iggy was simply lonely. It didn't have anything to do with me specifically, and I could prove it.

"You don't know me," I insisted. "Not really."

"Try me."

"What was my first car?" I asked.

His eyebrows came together. "You didn't have a car for a long time. You had a bicycle and then a motorbike. Your first car was probably the Lexus my father supplied when we lived in the States."

I swallowed. Lucky guess.

"And who was the first man I kissed?"

Iggy's signature cocky grin appeared. "That's easy. That wanker from Birmingham who tried to convince you to quit your job. You'd waited to hook up with another man all through the military and our time in the States only to end up with that sad sack."

"False. You don't know as much about me as you thought, Ignatius."

His eyes flared. "I didn't count the time I tried kissing you when I was in college. I was hardly a man at the time. Or so you said."

My face heated. I needed to get out of his room. Immediately. "And I was right." *Even though it remains the most beloved kiss in my memory because it was you.*

"Have dinner with me."

It wasn't a question but a command, and I longed to yield to it.

"No, thank you. Have a good evening, si—Iggy." I'd almost called him "sir," something I refused to do anymore...

At least outside of my fantasies.

I nodded awkwardly and left. When I made it safely into my own suite again, I let out a breath and clenched my hands into fists.

Why was he doing this? Why come here? Why ruin my great escape? For all his wealth and privilege, my Iggy had never been a spoiled brat.

He's also never been a liar.

I pushed that thought away. He couldn't possibly mean the things he was saying.

Could he?

I thought of the question I hadn't had the guts to ask Iggy when he'd tried to prove how well he knew me:

What would I do for love?

The answer was as wide as the ocean and as vast as the wild lands surrounding us as we raced through the South African night.

5

IGGY

He wasn't unaffected by me.

I twirled the thought through my mind as I made my way down the long, hushed corridors of the train to the dining car.

Jon's hands had trembled as he'd held my cuffs. His cheeks had flushed as they always did when he stood close. And the scent coming off his warm skin was the cologne I'd given him for his birthday last year.

He didn't believe I wanted him. That was the problem. He thought I was tagging along on his adventure from a selfish desire not to lose my valet.

It still stung like a bastard that he could misunderstand me so badly, but I could be patient.

It wasn't like I had a choice.

When I arrived in the dining car, I was taken to a table for two. The uniformed server removed the extra place setting with a sympathetic frown—*just in case I hadn't felt pathetically lonely already, thanks very much*—and I was halfway through my first martini when Jon walked past my table to the one ahead of mine.

I couldn't help but drink in the sight of him, something I'd consciously tried not to do in the past. I hadn't wanted Jon to feel uncomfortable, to see my longing for him and be unable to return it. In fact, I'd made a conscious effort not to speak to him much at all of late, to distract myself with other things and people as much as I could. I hadn't wanted to give him a reason to leave.

See how well that's worked out?

The server who sat him went through the same place setting removal and welcome spiel, leaving him sitting directly in front of me. Also alone.

"This is ridiculous," I told his broad back. "Come sit with me."

Jon's body stiffened until his shoulders were by his ears. "No."

"We've shared a thousand meals together." A thousand easy conversations where we'd talked each other's ears off, losing time telling each other stories or asking each other challenging questions about life and the world. "Why not one more?"

He stretched his head from side to side without responding.

"You know, Banks… I can help you with that tension problem of yours," I said, unable to help myself. Wanting to get under his skin the way he currently *lived* under mine. "Anytime. Just knock on my door. Day or night."

He didn't reply. Meanwhile, my words conjured a vision in my head, and I knew I'd be up all night wondering how easy it would be to break the lock on Jon's door and slide into bed beside him.

"Great, now you're a creep," I muttered to myself.

I took another healthy swig of the martini and wondered how long it would take for the server to bring the bottle of wine I'd ordered.

"If only I'd brought my phone," I said a bit louder. "If only a certain arsehole hadn't trained me that it was bad manners to bring my phone to dinner."

"*Live in the moment,*" Jon had said. "*Be present.*" But I didn't want to live in this moment if I couldn't talk to him or see his face.

"Wonder what that arsehole would say," I mused, "about the etiquette of not responding when someone is speaking to you."

Jon sipped his water calmly, and the bubbling cauldron of want and need in my gut threatened to boil over.

"Fuck this." I threw my napkin on the plate and shoved my chair back. I'd ask the server to send my dinner to my suite instead.

"Oh, for god's sake, Iggy," Jon said, turning around at last. "Come sit here, then, if you're going to be an idiot about it."

It was on the tip of my tongue to tell him to fuck off and take his prim, judgmental attitude with him. But I was too desperate for his company. I was willing to beg for scraps.

I grabbed my place setting and moved to his table. "What a lovely invitation. Don't mind if I do."

He glared at me. "The condition of you sitting here is to stop this spoiled-brat routine. Understand?"

And now we were back to him being my guardian rather than my friend? "Yes, *sir*."

Jon's eyes roved over my face. "You haven't been sleeping," he accused. "Christ, Iggy, you know a night at home once in a while wouldn't—" He shook his head once. "Why are you here?"

It took me a moment to find my voice. *Jon cared.* I hadn't realized how much I'd needed that confirmation. "At your table? You invited me."

He didn't answer. Instead, he did what he always did when he was unhappy with me. He waited me out until I started incriminating myself.

"I told you, I didn't know you'd be here," I began, dropping the fake cheer and sarcasm because it was exhausting. "Truly. I came because I remembered you talking about this train, and I..." I twisted my tongue inside my mouth, forcing it to say the words. "I wanted to be close to you. I missed you. *Not* the valeting. Not the managing. *You*, Jon. And I don't know how I fucked things up or what I did to make you leave, but if you'll come back with me, I'll do anything—"

"Anything?" Jon looked down at the fork he was fiddling with. "Then tell me, why haven't you had a serious relationship before?"

The question startled me, but I'd said *anything*. So, I'd be real with him, even if it scared him off. At least I'd know I'd given it—him, *us*—one last try.

I took a breath and laid my heart on the table between us. "I have been in love with the same man since I was fifteen. I would say four-teen, but I actually hated you a little at first. My father's spy. The fun police. It wasn't until I accidentally saw you with your shirt off that I realized how hard I could fall for a fun-killing prick."

Jon swallowed. "You hardly knew me."

"*Don't*," I snarled low. I didn't want to make a scene, but I wouldn't allow him to minimize what I felt for him. "I knew you. I've already proven that. I know you still."

His eyes widened, but he didn't argue. I continued. "You were happy to escape the army, get away from your family, lick your wounds where only a bunch of rich kids could see. I know you had nightmares from Iraq, saw things you wish you could erase from your memory. I loved you for that. For caring. For fighting. For being honest about it breaking you."

I met his eyes. "Then I watched you come back from it. I knew you talked to someone when we moved to Cambridge. You became lighter somehow. You smiled."

Jon looked back at the damned fork. "I shouldn't have told you any of that."

"Bullshit. You taught me that a man could define his own life. That I shouldn't compromise. I came out because of you. Found my passion because of you. You helped me build a life worth living. How could I not fall in love with you, Jon, even if I thought you'd never love me back?"

Jon sucked in a breath but still didn't meet my eyes, so I kept talking.

"I've been so terrified of scaring you off that I've tried my damnedest to put space between us. Even put space between me and every person who'd ask me about you. I've pretended to be carefree when I'm dying inside, to be sleeping around when I haven't fucked anyone in *months* because none of them are you. But you left anyway. And I realized it's not a life worth living if I can't be myself. If I can't have the man I love. So I'm not sorry that we're both on this train. I'm not sorry that I get a chance to tell you these things. Because you should know that you have my heart, even if you don't... if you can't..."

Jon's hand tightened around the fork, and I realized I was losing. Panicked, I blurted, "What would it take to convince you my feelings for you are real? That I know what I want?"

Jon looked up at last, and I was taken aback by the honesty in his eyes.

He wasn't ignoring me. He was terrified.

"You would have to stay with me forever and promise me you would never leave."

Tears simmered behind my eyes, threatening to fall. Could this be real? Was this happening?

After twenty fucking years, was Jonathan Banks finally going to give me a chance?

6

JON

Iggy stood and grabbed my hand, nearly tipping the table. Without sparing a glance at the diners around us or the poor servers who would have to deal with our aborted meal, he dragged me down the narrow corridor back to our train car.

Once he'd yanked me through the door to my suite, which was fractionally closer, he shoved me against the closed door. "Tell me this is real. Tell me you truly want this."

Before I could say yes, *fuck yes*, he added, "Tell me you're not going to have regrets," in a broken voice.

Emotion vibrated off him. Fear, concern... *love.*

Iggy didn't lie. He didn't change his mind when it came to the things that mattered most in his life. If he said he'd been months without sex, he had been. And if he said I had his heart...

I brought my hands up to caress the sides of his face. "I have been in love with you since you were nineteen years old. I would say eighteen, but I actually hated you a little at first. You were a spoiled brat with a big mouth."

Iggy's laugh sounded like a sob. "You still think that about me."

"True." I smirked. "But when you turned nineteen, you finally had the body of a man to make me forget."

He lunged forward then, crushing my mouth with his. I made an embarrassing sound, the kind someone makes after two decades of wanting something he couldn't have.

The kiss was every-fucking-thing. Power and raw hunger, tenderness and delicate care, and jaw-dropping love in every single breath.

His lips were firm and warm, and he tasted of crisp gin and lime. I wanted more of it. I wanted to sip at his lips and swallow entire moments of this.

My hands gripped the front of his dinner jacket, the fabric smooth and familiar against my fingers. How many times had I fantasized about this while smoothing his lapels?

"Don't hurt me," I croaked against his mouth.

Iggy pulled away, suddenly worried he was physically harming me. It took only a glance at my face before he realized what I'd meant.

"Hurting you would be like cutting out my own fucking heart, Jon. Don't you know how much I love you? How I want to spend my life with you? How I want to make you happy?"

The words washed over me then, clearing away the last of my fear. I wanted him as much as he seemed to want me. So what the hell was I waiting for?

I lurched awkwardly toward him, intent on another searing kiss. The noise he let out as our lips came together again was feral, like an animal finally released from a cage.

His body was a coiled spring, but his touch was tender and reverent. The way his thumbs skimmed my jaw, his nose brushed my cheek, his knee gently nudged my legs apart so he could get closer.

The cold wood of the door against my back had turned warm. The dim lighting was soft and intimate. The slight movement under our feet felt exotic and a little wild. We were somewhere in the sub-Saharan night, alone together on the brink of a new adventure.

Our best adventure.

As his hands moved, sliding my jacket off my shoulders, I realized I was the happiest I'd ever been. Finally, we were here together without the job between us. We could be equals. Partners.

Lovers.

For once, I pulled off his jacket without a single care for where it ended up. I yanked his shirt out of his trousers and shoved my hands underneath, relishing in the feel of his hot skin.

"Want you so much," I admitted into the side of his face.

"Thank fuck," he said on a laughing exhale. "I'm scared to death of disappointing you."

"The infamous playboy is afraid of letting me down in the sack?" I teased.

"I've never made love before."

Iggy had the ability to stop my breath. I stared at him while my brain slotted so many details into place. The careless attitude toward sex. The lack of serious relationships. The many times he'd only half-teased about wanting to be with me.

I'd never taken it seriously.

Until now.

"I love you," I said, surprising myself as much as I'd surprised him. But it was the raw truth, and I no longer wanted to deny it, deny *him*. "And I'm sorry I didn't believe you at first. I wanted it too badly to believe it could be real."

Iggy's eyes filled with tears that didn't spill. "I've waited my whole life to hear those words from you," he whispered.

I moved him toward the bed and lowered him onto the crisp, white bedding before taking my time removing every single piece of his clothing.

I'd done this for him a million times, but this time was so different. Every touch held twenty years of unspoken affection and a lifetime of love to come.

When he was finally fully naked, I began undressing myself slowly so I could watch the heat smolder in his eyes.

He was hard, cock jutting up thick and long. I could finally take the time to stare, to imagine the feel of it inside me... my mouth, my throat, my ass. I wanted him everywhere.

"Come here," he begged. His cheeks and neck were as red as his cock, and his eyes were undeniably hungry.

After I'd removed the last of my clothing, I crawled onto the bed from the bottom, dropping open-mouthed kisses inside his ankle, his knee, his thigh.

When I was close enough for Iggy's hands to reach into my hair, he took great delight in messing it up. "I've fantasized about holding your hair and choking you with my cock," he said in a voice rough with desire. "Messing up your perfectly styled hair and coming all over your fucking face."

To punish him for putting that hot image in my head, I nosed his sac before running the flat of my tongue up his shaft.

"Fucking fuck, Banks. *Fuck.*"

I took the head of his cock in my mouth and held it there, inhaling the musky scent of him and tasting the salty warmth of his precum.

Two could play at this game.

I pulled off him and dropped too-light kisses up his belly to his nipples before propping myself above him and lowering my voice to a sultry slide. "I've fantasized about you shoving me up against the fitting room mirror at Drake's and fucking me raw, your hand clamped tight over my mouth to keep me from shouting out your name for everyone to hear."

His eyes flitted back as if all the oxygen in his brain had been depleted, but his hands banded more tightly around my back to hold me close.

Iggy took a deep breath before flipping me over onto my back in one quick move. His hard cock ground against my inner thigh like a promise. "Do you want me to fuck you, Jon?" The words were a tease, a continuation of the game.

Rhetorical.

We both knew how it would be between us. One of the reasons we'd worked together in our roles for so long was because I was a natural submissive to him, and he thrived on dominating me. I would do anything for him, and he'd always made sure I'd wanted for nothing, that I was cared for and safe. Even when he'd thought that meant pulling away from me.

Our eyes locked together, and a million words flowed between us in the quiet room. The sound of our shallow breaths, the hard ragged thumping of two hearts on fire, and the silent begging of men who had so much to lose and everything to gain.

Iggy's mouth dropped to my collarbone, the tip of his tongue sliding against my skin until I forgot to breathe. He continued down my chest, sucking on each nipple before nipping them and moving down more. When he finally took my dick in his mouth, I tried to memorize the sight of it. Of his full lips stretched wide around my cock. Of his tongue laving eagerly and his hands still trying to roam everywhere.

Within moments, he'd pushed my thighs up over his shoulders and moved his mouth down until his hot tongue was circling my hole and sending my heart rate into the stratosphere.

"Oh god," I groaned, cursing and thrashing as my most tender skin felt the soft abrasion of his tongue and then the harsher abrasion of his stubbled chin.

After a few minutes of sucking and licking, he brought his fingers up to stretch me out until I was out of my mind with pleasure, with need, with stark desperation for release.

"Not yet," he murmured against me. "Not yet."

"Iggy," I begged, reaching down to try and yank at his hair.

He pinned me with his honey-flecked eyes. "Not. Yet."

I arched backward on the bed and squeezed the base of my dick.

I was nothing if not obedient.

7

IGGY

My brain was going to explode. I was naked in bed with Jon. I was fucking Jon. He was pliant and willing beneath my hands, beneath my tongue. He tasted like the world's greatest treat, sweet and salty and made just for me.

I needed a condom and lube, but they were in my own suite, and we were in Jon's room.

"Fuck," I said, climbing off him. "Do not move. I'll be right back."

"Bathroom," he blurted. "Toiletry kit. And stop glaring at me."

"I thought you weren't sleeping with anyone," I said stupidly, taking the two steps to bring me to the tiny bathroom, where I quickly grabbed what I needed.

"I wasn't. Yet. I was hoping to find someone to…"

Anger flared hot and sharp in my gut as I stared down at him. "I see. Someone to fuck who wasn't me. Someone to help you forget who you belonged to. Someone else to—"

Jon yanked me down again and cut off my anger and jealousy with more kisses. I could have kissed him for hours and hours and hours without needing more.

Liar. I wanted more. Much more.

When we were both hard and desperate again, biting out curses and humping against each other's sweat-slick skin, I grabbed for the lube and condom before suiting up.

"Tell me you're sure," I said again. So help me, if he even for one minute expressed regret after this, I wouldn't be able to survive it.

"Inside," he croaked. "Please."

I folded him in half and began to press inside his tight heat. Jon's body was incredible, perfect, *made for me.*

"Jon," I breathed. "Fuck. So tight."

"Go slow," he urged, blushing over how long it had been for him.

I ran a thumb against the pink splotch on one cheek. He was so damned beautiful. His dark hair was messy against the white sheets, and his skin was damp with our shared heat.

"I will love you until the end of time," I confessed into the shell of his ear. My hips rocked back and forth, earning ground inside of him. When I finally bottomed out, I let out a breath and stayed still to let him adjust.

His glassy eyes tried focusing on me. "Iggy, *please.*"

I pulled back and thrust several times until finding just the right angle. Jon arched his neck, cords set out in stark relief. I leaned in to nibble and lick them as I sped up my hips, and Jon met me thrust for thrust. This was entirely different from the sex I'd had in the past. It was full of meaning and promise.

How had I lived so long without this? The look on his face, the taste of his skin, the smell of his need... I was drunk with it.

"Want you to come," I said roughly. "Want you to feel good."

I could barely think with the way his body was clasping mine, but I remembered to reach for his cock, to stroke him in time to our bodies' rhythm. He made the most incredible noises and filled the space around us with his pending climax. I both wanted him to come and never wanted it to end.

The sound of my name on his tongue, spoken between gasping breaths, was enough to bring me to the edge. Jon's body contracted just as my orgasm hit, and I slammed myself balls-deep into him, holding him tightly and promising to any gods who would listen that

I would take care of this man forever if fate would just... let me keep him.

Let him be mine. Please.

When I finally had to pull out, he made a disgruntled noise. I pressed a kiss to his sweaty cheek and murmured for him to stay there while I disposed of the condom and cleaned us both up.

Jon watched me as I moved around the small space, servicing him for once. I wondered what he was thinking, whether he would ask me to leave or beg me to stay. Break my heart or take it gently into his own keeping.

After returning the cloth to the small bathroom, I stepped back into the bedroom and tried to read his mind.

His face split in a mischievous grin. "You're very awkward after sex. I never would have imagined."

For once, I wasn't in the mood for teasing. "Please let me stay."

The smile fell from his face. "I thought that was a given."

Air *whooshed* from my chest as I dove into the bed beside him and yanked him into my arms. "Thank fuck."

Jon lay with his head on my chest for a few minutes while unspoken words filled the air around us. Finally, I couldn't stand it any longer.

"I'm moving to Oxfordshire."

He sat up to face me. "What? Why?"

"My parents finally gave me the cottage. I'm going to continue my work, but I'll move there to oversee the renovations in my free time." I watched him closely. He loved my family's historic home in Oxfordshire.

"But... you love London," he argued. "Your social life. Your friends..."

"... are exhausting," I finished with a sigh. "I told you, I was trying to distract myself." I threaded our fingers together. "From a very inconvenient attraction to my very sexy valet." I nipped the tip of his finger with my teeth. "It didn't work. Besides, I think I'd prefer working with a view of a nice garden instead of the city noise."

Jon pinched his lip between his teeth. "Or... or I could oversee the renovations..."

I gripped his hand more tightly, but my voice was as gentle as I could make it. "Would you come to the cottage and be with me? Make it a home for us? Plant your garden and watch it grow with me?"

Jon's eyes filled. "I want that. But are you sure—"

I didn't let him finish that ridiculous question. Instead, I grabbed his face and kissed him before tumbling him down onto the bed beneath me and showing him with my lips and hands and body—and *love*—that he was mine and I was his.

As the train moved swiftly through the South African night, taking us closer to new adventures we could share together, I could honestly say I'd never been more sure of anything in my life.

EPILOGUE
JON

One year later

"I DON'T CARE if we're not technically related. I still say you look like me," the love of my life told his goddaughter, who was nestled in his arms as he sat beside me on a wrought iron bench in the autumn sunshine behind our cottage, our sheepdog at our feet. "Isn't that right, gorgeous? Which is why you should have been called Iggianna. Who names an innocent child Penelope Henrietta Winnie Wilde Grimaldi, anyway?"

Penny clasped Iggy's jumper in her chubby fists and chewed it, contemplating the question seriously. Then, without warning, the princess stiffened all four limbs simultaneously and let out a high-pitched shriek that echoed off the stone walls of the garden.

"See?" Iggy demanded, holding her out for someone else to take. "She's horrified! And you two call yourselves parents. Don't worry, love. You'll always be Baby Iggie to me."

Felix laughed. "I don't know if Penny looks like you," he said wryly, bending to claim his daughter, who immediately calmed in her daddy's arms. "But I definitely see similarities. Stubbornness, for example."

Iggy sputtered in disbelief. "I believe you mean *decisiveness*. Penny and I know what we want, and we make it happen." He turned to me in appeal. "Isn't that right?"

I thought about that morning. Our bed. His Ferragamo tie around my wrists and his cock in my mouth. My mouth tipped up in a smile I couldn't have held back if I tried... so I didn't. "You *are* very good at getting what you want."

The look Iggy sent me was hot enough to melt glass—more than hot enough to melt a valet-turned-cottage-renovation-coordinator directly into his loving arms, especially when he slipped his finger into my belt loop, tugged me closer, and dropped his arm over my shoulder.

"I was thinking it was the late nights that they had in common," Lio said, grinning at his husband. He paused the royal horsey ride he was giving his son to shoot Iggy a pointed smirk. "Or the periodically excessive drool."

"Papa, *go*," the toddler prince commanded, tugging on Lio's hair, and with a grin at his royal consort, Lio obediently trotted off.

Felix gave the pair a besotted smile, reminding me of the bumpy road they'd had to their own happy ever after.

I'd once thought that kind of love was unattainable for me, but now I lived it every day.

Felix turned to Iggy and snorted. "Uncle Jon says no more late nights around here. Uncle Iggy's boring now. Writing editorials about LGBTQ rights? Endowing a community center? *Engaged*?" He shot me a wink. As he danced Penelope away over the grass, he called over his shoulder, "Ladies and gentlemen, the notorious Ignatius Corbridge has settled down."

"*Pfft*." Iggy held me tighter. "That's absurd."

"Wellll." I tucked my tongue in my cheek. "You did get an award for that editorial..."

"Yes, but—"

"And you did ask me to marry you." I held up my hand to show off the gorgeous ring he'd commissioned for me. "Unless that was... someone else?"

"Definitely not," he growled, grasping my hand possessively.

I grinned. "So maybe not 'settled down.' Maybe just... settled."

"Maybe happier and more in love than I ever thought possible," he said softly, pressing a kiss to the top of my head. Then, in a firmer voice, he added, "But definitely never boring."

"Welll," I said again, teasing this time.

"If you doubt me, Banks," he warned, "I'll simply have to prove it to you. Over and over again."

The promise in his voice made me shiver. So I turned in his arms and whispered in his ear, "Yes, sir."

FLIRT

STEVIE'S PROLOGUE

My crush on Evan Paige started in sixth grade when Terrance "The Terror" Jackman pantsed me in front of an entire soccer team. It wasn't the first time something like that had happened. I'd already been the focus of school bullies for years, pretty much since I'd come out of the womb flamboyantly gay and unable to hide it.

As I'd stood there, gasping with an oncoming panic attack while desperately clutching at my tiny, terrified dick and raisin balls, the most beautiful creature had stepped in front of me and yanked my pants back up before I could even cry out for my mommy like my inner toddler demanded.

Not that crying for my mommy had ever done anything more for me than earning bonus tears, but still. I'd been humiliated.

"What the hell is going on here?" my hero's deep voice boomed. Suddenly, instead of a team full of bullies, there were thirty angels staring at us with halos of innocence spinning lazily over their heads.

"Nothing, Coach Paige," Terrance said. "Steven's just so skinny, his pants fell down."

"And I'm the queen of England. Go sit in Coach Castillo's office until I come for you. Now."

After shooting me a menacing look behind his coach's back, Terrance took off for the cement-block recreation building on the far side of the field. The other kids shuffled around until the coach barked at them to get back to a dribbling exercise they were supposed to be doing. They took off running like a unified pack.

A pack of wolves. Rabid ones.

When he turned back to me, the coach's face softened. I looked up into kind gray eyes, a stubbled jaw I'd never have, and one of those chin dimple things that made him look like a Disney character. His thick, dark hair had some wave to it, and I remember wondering what it would feel like to touch it.

"Are you okay?" he asked in a gentle voice, as if I were a baby rabbit he might accidentally scare off.

I coughed a bit to make sure my voice didn't crack when I answered. "Yes... yes, sir. I'm fine."

"What are you doing out here by yourself?"

I looked over at the kids in their soccer shorts and brand-name Dri-FIT tops. Each of them wore the kind of popular athletic socks that cost almost ten bucks a pair. I looked at myself. I wore my brother's hand-me-down Hanes sweatpants from Walmart, tube socks that came ten in a pack, from the same, and a faded Care Bears T-shirt I'd lucked out in finding at Goodwill the previous summer. Of course, it still fit a year later. I was destined to stay the size of a fourth grader for the rest of my life.

Clearly I wasn't part of the team.

"I, uh... I was supposed to bring lunch for my brother. He works for Coach Castillo."

The large man looked around until he spotted the shredded brown paper bag several feet away on the ground. Kade's ham sandwich lay in its baggie on the grass, and the apple had obviously rolled over the baggie of pretzels, crushing at least half of them. The condensation from the water bottle had wetted the bag enough to break open a hole when the bag had hit the ground.

Kade was going to kick my ass.

"Here, let me help you gather this up," he said, kneeling down to collect the items. I couldn't help but notice the muscles in his back moving under the thin fabric of his shirt... or the rounded tightness of his butt, clearly the *result of playing so much soccer... or the dark hairs covering his shapely legs beneath the slippery fabric of his shorts...*

"Stevie!"

I snapped back to reality and saw my brother rushing across the field toward us.

"Oh shit," I muttered before remembering I was cursing in front of an adult. "Uh, sorry. That's... that's my brother, so I'll just..." I held out my hands for the items he'd picked up. It was an awkward transfer since there wasn't a bag to put it in. I finally had to pull out the hem of my T-shirt to make a kind of hammock for them until I could give them to Kade. "Thanks for... thanks," I said before turning and making my way across the grass.

Sure enough, Kade kicked my ass. But not there in front of my new crush. Later, at home before Mom got back from work. After I'd asked who the tall handsome coach was.

"You stay the fuck away from Coach Paige, you got me?" he'd growled. "Nobody wants your pansy ass mooning over the soccer coach. It's bad enough people know you're my brother—I don't need you coming around where I work and making a spectacle of yourself."

Yeah, my brother was a peach. He'd made sure when he'd grabbed me, my Care Bears shirt hadn't survived the pummeling.

After that, I'd been reduced to catching glimpses of Coach Paige from a distance. During summers when I was able to skulk around the soccer fields without Kade discovering me, I'd done so. During the school year when I'd learned he wasn't just a summer coach in Valley Cross but a school team coach in nearby Hobie, I'd managed to sneak away to some of their games.

I'd learned more about him. His name was Evan, and he was almost twenty years older than I was.

He was straight.

He'd dated a woman named Sierra, and I remember thinking how exotic she'd sounded. I'd stayed up at night in my top bunk and imagined what it looked like when Coach Paige had sex with Sierra. Was he sweet and gentle with her or hot and rough? Did he like her breasts, or was there any way he'd prefer a flatter chest? *If there is a god*, I remembered thinking, *please let him be an ass man.*

One time Sierra had showed up at a game. Coach had wrapped his chiseled arm around her narrow waist and kissed her on the cheek. I hadn't been able to help but daydream about being the one who stood in his strong embrace, the one who made him smile and laugh. He'd begun to take on a larger-than-life appearance in my mind. I fantasized about him being my everything. Taking care of me, protecting me, and even making some of my decisions for me when life got to be too much. He was like a mental touchstone. Whenever I'd found myself the victim of bullying at school or my brother's foul moods at home, I'd imagined Evan Paige coming to my rescue again, swooping me up in his giant embrace and keeping me safe from the rest of the world.

But of course, that had never happened.

Until the night I turned eighteen and bought my first *Playgirl* magazine from the corner store just because I could. I'd happily masturbated myself into a stupor, accidentally leaving the magazine visible on the floor. Of course, my brother had seen it as soon as he came home. Once he'd taken out his frustrations on my face, Kade had barricaded me in my room and gone into a rage that resulted in him throwing shit around, including a kitchen towel that had landed on the hot stove, accidentally setting fire to the apartment.

EVAN'S PROLOGUE

THE FIRST TIME I saw Stevie Devore, he couldn't have been more than eleven or twelve and had just been pantsed by a bully attending one of my summer soccer camps. The poor kid had stood there, grabbing his junk in horror while the group of bullies snickered at him. I'd helped as best I could, hiding him from view while I yanked his shorts back up, but the damage had been done. Not only had he been humiliated, but I'd heard a rumor that he'd also been teased by his very own brother for it later that night. His older brother, Kade, had worked for my boss at the rec center in Valley Cross that summer and had been a total piece of work. Lazy, entitled, and bigoted. The very idea of that little middle schooler in the cartoon T-shirt and hand-me-down Walmart sweatpants being related to cocky Kade Devore set my teeth on edge.

If I was being honest with myself, my desire to watch over Stevie had started all the way back then, almost ten years ago. But I didn't see him again until seven years later, when I'd responded to an apartment fire in nearby Valley Cross. I'd ascended the ladder to help someone from a two-story apartment window and encountered a familiar face. Only this time it was black and blue and covered in soot.

"What happened?" I asked the gangly teen as I reached in the window to help him climb out. From what I'd gathered, he was trapped in the bedroom of the very apartment where the blaze originated.

He was trembling like a leaf and seemed scared out of his mind. "My b-brother," he stammered through tears. "He... he was angry, and he..." He hiccupped and reached for me with skinny arms left bare in a tank top. He had on some kind of colorful pajama bottoms too, but that was it. It was winter. The poor guy was going to freeze.

"Oh, honey," I murmured, pulling the kid close to make sure he didn't fall from the ladder. "Did he hurt you?"

My words only made him cry harder. Once we made it safely onto the ground and away from where the rest of the crew battled the fire, I wrapped a Mylar blanket around him and found a spare pair of boots in the truck for him to put on before taking him to the back of the bus to check out his injuries.

"There's a big accident west of town that has the Valley Cross responders busy. I'm afraid the Hobie fire crew is all you've got, but I'm also an EMT, so I should be able to help you out here."

I used some wipes to gently clean the smudges off his face so I could see what was actual bruising. Even with the blanket wrapped tightly around the kid, he shivered violently.

"What's your name?" I asked softly.

"S-Stevie," he replied through chattering teeth.

"We've met before. Do you play soccer?" I moved the blanket aside enough to slip the blood pressure cuff onto his arm.

"N-no," he said, turning his face away from me. "I g-graduated. B-b-but I've been t-to some of the g-games."

"You didn't go to school in Hobie, did you?"

He shook his head. "V-Valley Cross."

"Have a friend on the Hobie team?"

Stevie's eyes looked up at me with such sadness, such vulnerability, I suddenly remembered. He was the boy who'd been bullied while bringing his brother lunch at the soccer fields. My heart clenched. This poor guy and his jackass of a brother.

"You said your older brother did this? Kade, right?" I asked.

Stevie's eyes widened at the name as if he was surprised I knew who his brother was. "N-no, I was c-confused. It was an-n-n accident." He began coughing violently, and I reached for the oxygen mask.

His hair was a tangle of dirty, dyed-green spikes, made messier by the smoke and the trauma of his experience. Once I settled the mask on his face, I brushed his hair back from his eyes. "Shh, just take it easy. Slow breaths."

He did as I said and began to relax finally, slumping sideways a bit until he was leaning heavily against me.

"Lieutenant Paige, what've we got?" the chief's voice called out from across the parking lot as he strode toward me.

Stevie jerked up and pulled away from me, shooting me a guilty look for some reason. I reached over and squeezed his hand to reassure him it was fine. All victims needed support and comfort.

I tried not to admit to myself that my desire to comfort and support this particular victim was considerably stronger than normal for some reason. I wasn't attracted to him sexually—he was barely legal, and I was twice his age—but he seemed to need me... to need someone *on his side, and I couldn't handle the idea of him not having what he needed.*

As I explained what I knew of Stevie's condition, my boss's radio squawked. Before I could do more than assure Stevie he didn't have any serious injuries besides the facial bruises his asshole brother had given him, Stevie's mother approached with a toddler on her hip and began fussing at him.

"Why didn't you come out of that room when I yelled for you? This poor fireman had to use the ladder to save you. Who do you think you are, some kind of pretty princess? If you'd just come out when Kade told us to go, we could have avoided all this drama. You just have to be the center of attention, don't you?" She reached for his arm just when the chief's radio squawked again.

I heard enough through the radio to know the chief was going to send me to an accident back in the direction of Hobie. The last thing I wanted to do was leave this poor kid with his terrible mother, but I had to remind myself he was safe while the victims of the car accident weren't. I leaned into the truck and pulled out a scrap piece of paper, quickly jotting my number down. When I handed it to Stevie, I met his eyes and tried to get across how serious I was. "Call me if you need anything. Okay? And tell the officer what really happened in there."

He nodded and took the piece of paper, curling his fingers around it before his mother led him back toward the group of apartment residents on the other side of the lot.

There hadn't been anything I could do, really. Once the fire was out, it had been a matter for the Valley Cross police. As disappointing as it was to discover later that his brother hadn't been charged with assault from the night of the fire, I understood sometimes justice didn't prevail, especially in cases involving domestic issues.

I hadn't heard from Stevie again, so I'd assumed all was well even though something deep in my gut had told me otherwise.

A year later I saw for myself.

One day I'd wandered into the little bakery on the Hobie square for a coffee and had seen him behind the counter. He'd looked completely different than the kid I'd rescued from the apartment fire. He was happy and healthy and overwhelmingly himself. I'd become a regular customer after that and found myself looking forward to seeing his smiling face every day. As he'd gradually let go of his shyness around me, I'd seen the energetic, flamboyant, beautiful person he was as an adult.

Part of me had breathed a sigh of relief that first day I'd seen him in the bakery. I remembered thinking he'd made it. He'd gotten out of his oppressive family situation and found a way to be happy. His cheerful personality was absolutely stunning, and I looked forward to his flirty smile every day. I'd still seen him as a kid, naturally, until one night last summer when I'd caught him eyeing me with a certain look on his face.

I'd been out on a date with a woman named Jolie once or twice already, and that night would have been a tipping point from us having a couple of meals together to actually dating if it hadn't been for that single glimpse of Stevie. Jolie and I had been seated at a small table by the big picture window looking out onto the Hobie town square, and the night had been alive with happy couples and families enjoying the June weather.

After ordering our food, Jolie had lifted her wineglass for a toast. "To finding that special spark," she'd said with a lovely smile. I'd never forget those words because right after taking the sip of wine, I'd locked eyes with Stevie Devore through the restaurant window and found a *real* spark—one I'd never even come close to feeling before.

The look on his face as his eyes flicked between Jolie and me had been different than ever before. Disappointed, jealous... *possessive.*

It had reached right into my chest and squeezed my heart to the point I could barely take another breath.

That was the moment "little Stevie Devore" suddenly became not so little. And in a way, that's when our coming together became inevitable.

1

STEVIE

Late January

"CHRIST ON A CRAWDAD, what the fuck is that?" I was trying super hard not to slur, but it was a near thing.

"Is... is... mega birthday drink." My best friend, Sassy, giggled before sloshing the giant pink drink in front of me. The fruit sword and paper umbrella tumbled out onto the rough wooden tabletop with a plop. "For the birthday boys... boysss... *boy*."

I narrowed my eyes at her, trying to combine the multiple Sassy's into one proper Sassy. I'd already had many, many mega birthday drinks. "You tryna get me drunk?"

"Tryna get you *laid*," she corrected with a hiccup. "'Bout time you had your cherry popped."

"Shhh," I hissed at her, glancing around to make sure no one overheard her. "Shut the fuck up. It's a secret, you skank. I have a reputation to uphold."

"Best-kept secret in Hobie, Texas," she hollered to anyone who would listen. Thankfully, we weren't in Hobie at the moment. We were in Dallas at a gay dance club with hot-as-fuck go-go boys. Because my best friend loved me.

"I'm going to dance. If I drink any more of that shit, I'm going into diabetic shock." I made my way to the dance floor and lost myself in a sea of glorious male bodies. The alcohol had stripped away what little inhibition I had, and my body began to move to the music the way it did when I was alone behind closed doors. I danced my fucking heart out, losing time to the sweaty pleasure of moving to the rhythm of a bass beat.

I'd waited so long to be able to come to one of these clubs, and now I was finally old enough. Thank Goddess my younger bestie had a sister who'd let her borrow her ID for the night. My older brother would have never let me borrow his, especially if he'd known why I'd wanted it.

I looked around at all the sexy men. Nope, Kade would have rather thrown himself on a land mine than help his sissy brother dance with a bunch of pansies. A sigh escaped my lips.

They were such beautiful pansies. The most pretty pansies ever. And I was one of them, happily moving my body along with theirs in the flashing lights.

At one point, Sassy joined me with a flushed face and eyes full of mischief.

"What?" I yelled over the music.

"They love you," she cried. "No one can keep their eyes off you."

"Pfft." I ignored her and spun around, shaking my ass in her face and raising my arms up above my head. I didn't think anything of her comment, just a birthday nicety by my boo, until I took a break and made my way back toward the bathroom.

A man in a suit approached me with a big smile. "You have great moves."

"Thanks," I said, checking him out. He was a little too slick and polished for my taste, but I appreciated his attempt. "All those hours of watching YouTube are finally paying off." I went to move past him, but he called out for me to wait.

"Have you ever thought about making money with those moves? We're hiring more dancers right now if you're interested." He pulled a card from his back pocket and handed it to me. "My name is

Darius. I'm the assistant manager here, and I'd love to see you at one of our auditions. I can't promise anything until I see more, but I've got to tell you, the guys couldn't stop staring at you on the dance floor."

I probably stood there for a beat too long with my jaw hanging open. I'd assumed he was coming on to me, not approaching me with a job lead.

"You're kidding. Did Sassy put you up to this?" I asked, craning my neck to see if she was hiding somewhere with her phone recording the prank.

He flashed an easy smile and pressed a business card into my hand. The graphic on the front matched the branding of the newish club called Feathers. "No, I don't know who that is. But I promise this is for real. The audition schedule and details are posted under the jobs tab on our website. Check it out and see what you think. Call me with any questions."

As he moved back into the club, I stared after him.

Fuck, I must have been way drunker than I thought. For a minute there, I thought someone had just propositioned me to become a stripper.

Even if it was something I'd never have the guts to even consider, just being asked made this the best birthday ever. And I had to admit, that kind of money sure would make my hourly wage at the bakery look like chump change.

I shook my head with a laugh before proceeding to the men's room and promptly forgetting all about it when I returned to Sassy and my millionth mega birthday drink.

Two days later, I realized I must have inadvertently spilled the beans about the audition offer to Sassy while I was still drunk that night.

"You should do it," she said from her spot at the end of the counter in the bakery where I worked. "You'd be so good at it, and the tips would be incredible. Plus, you'd be able to sign Willow up for dance lessons that much quicker."

"Keep your voice down. And, did you forget that those guys are pretty much *naked* while they're dancing?" I hissed, even though she was right. The idea of being able to get my little sister into the dance lessons she'd been begging for was almost worth considering becoming a stripper for.

"What guys?" Nico asked from behind me, scaring the shit out of me and causing me to scream bloody murder.

"Jesus, take the wheel, my heart!" I cried, clutching at my chest. "Stop fucking doing that, you asshole."

My boss just grinned at me. "I love sneaking up on you and hearing you screech like Pippa. Warms my cockles."

I gritted my teeth. "Yeah, well, next time it's gonna do something else to your cockles."

"Seriously though," Sassy continued as if I hadn't just experienced myocardial infarction while rearranging cookies on a tray. "You should at least audition."

Before I had a chance to tell her to shut the hell up again, Nico piped up. "Audition to be a naked dancer? Do tell. I'm intrigued."

"Perv," I muttered.

"Hey, that's my husband you're calling a perv," West said from the doorway to the kitchen. Oh great, more witnesses. Perf. "Not that he's not a perv, because he totally is. What are we talking about?"

"Nothing," I said at the same time Sassy said, "Stripping."

I whipped my head around. "It's not stripping!"

It was stripping.

"What's not stripping?" a deep voice asked, accompanied by the familiar tinkle of the bell over the bakery door.

Chief Paige. As in, hottest silver fox in all of Texas, Chief Paige. Firefighter, muscle man, Hobie's hero, and all-around dreamboat. Otherwise known (although only to me) as My One and Only. The solo coin in my spank bank.

I bit back a dreamy sigh and forced myself to speak first to shut this shit down before anyone else clued him in to the topic at hand.

"Stripping paint off an old dresser," I squeaked in a wholly unmanly octave. "I was thinking about a craft project. You know, glitter, gems, decals... that sort of thing. But first I have to get the old layers of paint off. Any suggestions?"

West, Nico, and Sassy all stared at me, and I glared back at them with an *I dare you* warning on my face. At least, I hoped that's what the message said.

Sassy, goddess love her, got the message. Praise the baby Jesus for besties.

"Yes, Stevie found this god-awful thing at the thrift store in Valley Cross and doesn't know the first thing about refinishing it," she said.

I owed the woman a foot massage.

"Oh, well, I've refinished several things at the lake house. I'm happy to teach you a thing or two, if you'd like," Chief Paige said, moving closer to the counter where I stood. His gorgeous gray eyes were so damned kind. I wanted to dive into them and swim around until all of the orgasms happened.

"He'd love that," Nico blurted loudly, right next to my ear.

I jumped and spun around to kick him in the shins. "Stop that, you dick! I swear to *good gravy*, the next time you startle me, I'm going to—"

"Yes," Sassy said quickly, meeting my eye. "Lord knows *someone* needs to teach him about stripping. Contrary to popular belief, the boy has no experience with that sort of thing."

I felt all the blood rush from my face. Did she... did she just say what I thought she said?

Chief Paige chuckled in his deliciously panty-dropping deep voice. "I can get off this weekend if that works for you, Stevie?"

"I... I..." I stammered at the beautiful creature before me. "I would love for you to get off this weekend. And I would love for *me* to get off this weekend. We could both get off together... that would be even better... us getting off, I mean. Together."

Nico looked at me with confusion. "You already got off this weekend. It's on the calendar."

West and Sassy burst out laughing. "I don't think that's what he meant," West whispered to his husband.

Thank fuck the chief was too busy looking at the pastries and cookies in the display to notice what was going on.

"S-sounds good, Chief," I said. "I'll... I'll just come to your place Saturday morning, then?"

He looked up and graced me with one of his full grins, the kind that deepened the chin dimple and crinkled his eyes. "Perfect. Be sure to wear clothes that can be destroyed."

"Uh-huh," I breathed.

"Oh, and Stevie?"

"Uh-huh?"

"Call me Evan."

Merciful heavens. I wondered if the precum leaking out of me could be seen through the layers of thong, skinny jeans, untucked sequined T-shirt, and ugly-ass bakery apron. If Goddess gave a shit about me, the answer would be no.

It was all something out of a dream come true until he said the fatal words before walking out of the bakery with his coffee and cookie.

"If you have any friends who want to tag along, feel free to bring them. It's been a while since I've had a youth group at my place. Maybe I'll pick up some sodas and snacks. Oh, and bring swimsuits. You can all go for a dip off the dock after."

That cocky-ass motherfucker thought I was a kid.

I stared after him as he sauntered his gorgeous butt out of Sugar Britches. The minute the door closed behind him, I turned to Sassy with smoke pouring from my nose and ears.

"Gas up the car. We're going to Dallas for that audition."

If that old man wanted to think of me as some at-risk youth from his volunteering gigs, he was going to get the shock of his life when he learned I was waving around my very adult-sized cock for cash.

I'd spent three years trying to get that man's attention by flirting with everyone in town. The fact he still thought of me as the little kid he'd once saved from a bully, and later, the apartment fire, made me mad as hell.

And hell hath no fury like a Stevie scorned.

2

EVAN

I LEFT the bakery in much better spirits than I'd entered it. Getting under Stevie Devore's skin was one of my favorite pastimes. Maybe it was cruel of me to mess with him by implying he was a kid, but he was so damned adorable when he got angry. His cheeks flushed, his little hands balled into fists at his sides, and his nostrils flared.

Stevie in full pique was a sight to behold. He was lovely on a normal day, but when ticked off? Ahh, that's when he made my heart stutter-step and thunk like a lovesick fool.

Stopping by Sugar Britches for a coffee and cookie had become a daily habit of mine since I'd discovered Stevie working there a couple of years before. At the time, I truly had thought of him as a kid, because I'd actually known him as one. But by now it had been a good eight months of seeing him as the man he was.

I was very aware of the fact he'd finally turned twenty-one. I hadn't let myself spend too much time fantasizing about the beautiful boy until he was old enough to have a glass of wine with me on our first date, but now it was time to finally make my move.

And I was going to enjoy every minute of it.

The plan to teach him how to refinish furniture had been a fortuitous one. It would take several hours a day over many days with the two of us alone in the workshop off the back of my garage. Despite Stevie's propensity to bring bakery treats to the fire house on occasion and my regular stop-ins for coffee, we'd never really had a chance to spend any time just the two of us.

It was time for that to change.

When I got home, I quickly changed into some old clothes and made my way out to the workshop, cranking up some loud rock on my Bluetooth speakers to keep me company. There were piles of tools and half-finished projects lying around, so I spent a couple of hours tidying up and organizing the large space. Once I was done, there was room for his dresser, and the first few items we'd need for paint stripping were laid out on a workbench.

Later that night I received an email inviting me to a bachelor party of sorts for an old friend who'd worked on a special wildfire response crew a few years back. There were ten of us on the crew who'd been through some shit together at the time, and even after we'd gone our separate ways, we'd kept in touch.

Weekend after next, we were all apparently taking Cody to a new club so he could enjoy plenty of drinks, dancing, and dick before taking the plunge with his partner, Eric. I grinned at the image of a table full of firefighters at a gay club. Two of the men in our group would squirm uncomfortably the entire time, and I couldn't wait to give them hell about it. There was no chance they'd let their discomfort keep them from joining us to celebrate Cody, and for that I was grateful. It was a pretty damned decent group of men I was thankful to know.

I responded *hell yes* to the invite and closed down my laptop to get ready for bed. I was covering a twenty-four-hour shift for one of my men starting tomorrow, and I needed to get some sleep in order to be at full strength. The long shifts weren't getting easier now that I was well into my forties, but if I didn't eat and drink a bunch of unhealthy crap and made sure to get enough sleep, I could handle it as well as any other firefighter in the house.

The following day went by in a flash. We had an inspection scheduled at the pub Hudson Wilde was helping get off the ground, and there were several streets of hydrants that needed regular maintenance. The Texas winter weather was the good kind of cold. Sunshine kept everyone's moods up, and the chilly air was the perfect counter to our sweaty work. By the time I got off that shift, I had a full day's work of my own to get through, which left me utterly exhausted Wednesday night when I crawled home and put myself to bed.

I slept late on Thursday, which pissed me off because Stevie only worked mornings on Thursdays. By the time I'd woken up, it was too late to catch a glimpse of my favorite bakery boy at Sugar Britches, so I consoled myself with a big omelette breakfast at home followed by an extensive jacking-off session with visions of Stevie Devore riding me, hips undulating, needy noises spilling from his throat and his gorgeous slender form covered in delicious naked skin hungry for my touch.

When I heard tires crunch on the gravel drive, I startled out of my cum-covered haze and quickly made my way to the bathroom to clean up before seeing who the hell was stopping by on a random Thursday afternoon.

3

———————

STEVIE

"Cocksucking son of a bitch," I muttered, elbowing my way past overfull racks of musty old clothes in search of a dresser that needed stripping. "Calling me a child. I'll show him who's a fucking child, motherfucker."

"Excuse me?" The older gentleman behind the counter of the thrift store reached for his bow tie as if my words were choking him.

"Not you, dear," I assured him in my sweetest voice. "No offense, but you don't seem the cocksucking type."

Sassy's light snort came from somewhere over to my right.

"This is all your fault, McSassafrass," I snapped. "Had you not—"

"Save it, princess," she said. "It's been three days since the youth group comment. Pull an Elsa and let it go. Oh! I found one. Over here."

I almost tripped over a plastic crate of old vinyl records before coming to a sudden stop in front of the strange, avocado-colored monstrosity.

"That's... what is that?" I asked.

The older man from the counter sauntered over with his hands clasped behind his back. "Ahh, that is an antique Dutch bombe commode. Fully restored it would be the pride of anyone's dining room, and it's quite sufficient enough to hold a nice Belgian lace collection."

I narrowed my eyes at his snobbery. The man worked in a shit shop for god's sake. The funny-shaped chest of drawers had a tag on it that claimed the thing was twenty bucks. "And how well would it hold, oh, let's say... a nice *dildo* collection?"

The man's eyes probably weren't supposed to get that big. It didn't seem healthy.

Sassy stepped on my toe and flashed the man a brilliant smile. "He means PreMo... you know? Precious Moments? That's what all the young kids are calling those lovely collectibles nowadays. Stevie here has loads of them. He's especially enamored with his 'God Loveth A Cheerful Giver' one, aren't you, dumpling?"

For some reason, the man's eyes glazed over in rapturous splendor. "You have that one? Oh my-lanta, isn't the little girl with the wagonload of Cavalier spaniels just charming? Would you ever think about selling it?"

"Oh, ah, sure. What's it worth? Couple bucks?" I turned to Sassy and gave her the *this guy's a psycho* look.

The man laughed. "Silly you. No, but I can give you three hundred for it if it's in good condition. You two make a sweet couple. For a minute there, I thought maybe you were... well, you *know*."

Now my eyes were the ones bugging. I ignored his ignorance as best I could. "Three hundred? Jiminy-bigots, that's a lot of cash for a white girl and her chattel."

I could feel Sassy's entire body vibrating with silent laughter.

"We'll think on that, Gerald," I said, wondering what his name really was. "In the meantime, I think we want this dildo display case if you don't mind. Saskatoon, sweetheart, your handcuffs will fit in the center drawer, don't you think?"

"Powder puffs!" Sassy blurted. "Yes, my powder puffs will fit in there just beautifully, darling."

Sassy turned and smacked me in the stomach. I winked at Gerald. "Don't listen to a word she says. This one's a tiger in bed, make no mistake."

~

BY THE TIME we made our way back to Hobie with the giant green dresser in the back of the pickup truck Sassy had borrowed from her Grandpa, I was a good three hours past my freshness date. It was Thursday, which meant I needed to shake a tail feather if I wanted to make it to my night shift job at the hospital without looking like a wilted salami.

"I need a shower," I whined. "I'm really too pretty to lift things and end up so... *moist.*" I shuddered.

"You can shower after we drop this monster off at the chief's house," Sassy said, blowing a dark curl off her forehead. If I thought I was a sweaty mess, she was ten times worse. I had to admit, I'd kind of phoned it in when it was time to do the heavy lifting. She may not have minded breaking a nail, but I wasn't about to risk my own on that monstrosity.

Her words sank in, causing me to gasp. "Oh hayel no. We are not going there until I have a chance to reboot. This situation," I said, waving a palm around my general person, "needs at least two hours of—"

A brownish blur flashed in front of the truck.

"Shit! What was that?" Sassy screeched, swerving to avoid hitting whatever it was.

I grabbed the dash and whipped around in my seat to see what it was. "Stop the truck! I think it's a dog."

Before she'd even put the truck in park, I was out the door, racing to see if the animal was okay. It wasn't a dog. It was a giant brown catlike thing the size of a dog.

"What the fuck have you been eating, sweetheart?" I murmured, reaching for the stunned animal. It looked like it was more scared than hurt, but I approached it cautiously regardless. Sticking your hand out at a scared cat was equivalent to reaching into a blender and hoping the thing didn't power on.

The cat let out a pitiful mew and waddled toward me, rubbing its pink nose against my outstretched hand before winding itself through my legs.

"Let's not go crazy," I warned the dirty thing. "These are Abercrombie jeans. Just because I stole them from my best friend, doesn't mean I want you getting your manky fur all over them."

"I thought those looked familiar. It's not fair they look better on you than me," Sassy said, leaning halfway out the driver's-side window. "Load him in the truck and let's go."

"What? No. I'm not touching this nasty thing," I said defiantly, reaching for the cat and pulling it against my chest.

"Sure you're not. You and I both know you can't resist an animal in need. And hey, maybe this time you won't get it knocked up."

She turned to walk back to the truck while I scrambled to follow, tucking the big fat fattie against my cardigan. Thank god the twinset I had on had come from the thrift store. I could burn it later and not feel bad.

"That was *one* time, Sassington! One time I got a dog knocked up. I can't believe you can't let a little thing like that go. We don't even know yet if she's actually preggo. It just happened last weekend for goddess's sake."

"It's a champion trial dog. The puppies are worth—"

"Stop," I groaned. "I know. We've been over this. Did I tell you he took me to dinner last night?"

"Who, Charlie?" she asked in surprise.

"Yeah. Sweet little Irish sexpot." I batted my eyes at her as I chucked the skanky hoss in the back seat of the truck.

"Dude, I know who Charlie is. Why didn't you tell me he asked you out?"

I shrugged and began searching through the truck's pockets and glove box for napkins to wipe kitty cooties off me. No luck. "It was a dud. We went to Nonna's for Italian, and... I don't know. I couldn't stop comparing him to Chief Hot Stuff."

Sassy turned to look at me after she pulled back out onto the road. "Babe, you've got it bad. If you couldn't make things work with the lovely Irish guy... man, that's really something."

I rolled my eyes and faced away from her, watching the barren winter fields pass by as Sassy made her way toward the secluded lake property where Chief Paige lived.

"It's stupid is what it is," I muttered. "Maybe I'll meet some hot go-go dancer at the club."

"Did you find out yet when Darius wants you to come in for the audition?"

Nerves roiled in my gut at the thought of exposing myself to a club full of horny men. If any of them found out I was fresh, virginal meat... well, let's just say I'd considered Amazon-Priming myself some kind of chastity plug just in case. Knowing me, it would only make me horny the whole time, which they'd be able to see and/or smell on me. I would be like slathering a dog toy in peanut butter and tossing it in the show ring at Westminster.

By the time Sassy pulled the truck into Chief... *Evan's* driveway, I'd worked myself into full froth imagining being so irresistible on stage that all the sexy boys would chase me into the parking lot after my dancing shift.

"I think I've been reading too many gay harem books," I muttered. "I think I need to get one of those Husband and Husband cartoon books I keep seeing on social media instead. Those two are so stinking cute."

"What are you going on about?" Sassy called out from the far side of the truck where she'd begun untying the straps around the green dragon.

"Those cute Husbands," I said, speaking up so she could hear me. "I need to get one—" Before I had a chance to finish the sentence, I slammed the truck door closed and turned right into a hard, bare chest. "Holy hot chicken on a biscuit," I breathed. "That... that's a pectoral." My hand might have cupped said pec just to be sure.

"Steven," the deep rumbly voice said. "This is a pleasant surprise."

"I bought a dildo dresser," I blurted.

The silver fox blinked down at me. "That's... something."

I heard a feminine sigh from the other side of the truck. "Seriously. I can't even."

"I mean," I gasped. "I bought a green dragon that could hold dildos... if you wanted."

Sassy sighed again. "For the love of all that's holy, *stop*."

"N-no," I stammered, digging myself in deeper. "That's not what I meant. I meant it's a commode. A bombe commode. Dutch. A Dutch one... I mean, it's a Dutch bombe commode, whatever that is. And it's green. Well, it's not supposed to be green. That's why it was only twenty bucks. I think I could have negotiated it down a bit if Sassy hadn't gotten foul-mouthed with Gerald. But Gerald said—"

Sassy's slender hand covered my mouth from behind. "Stop talking right this minute," she hissed into my ear. "Trust me on this, big guy."

I blinked up at Evan. His eyes twinkled with laughter. The jerk probably couldn't help but laugh at the little pipsqueak stammering like an idiot.

"Let go of his nipple, Stevie," Sassy said slowly, reaching around me to pull my hand away from the bronzed chest muscles I was savoring.

"I don't want to," I whimpered.

Evan's eyes locked on mine. "The feeling is mutual."

My arm froze in place, and I felt Sassy stiffen behind me. Evan's grin turned feral.

"But if you touch mine, seems only fair I get to touch yours," he rumbled.

"Anddd... I'm out," Sassy said. Within three seconds she'd dropped the green dragon into the yard, chucked an overly fat cat onto the grass next to it, and peeled out of the driveway.

I stared after her.

"She just left me here."

A pair of large, warm hands cupped my cheeks. "Lucky me," Evan murmured.

And then he fucking kissed me.

4

EVAN

I couldn't wait another second to taste those full, sassy lips. I'd been fantasizing all week about finally getting my hands and mouth on Stevie Devore, and I'd even emptied my balls only moments ago to the image of doing so.

Stevie let out a squeak of surprise when I leaned in and kissed him. His eyes were as big as dinner plates, and his skin pinked up beautifully with a blush. I slid my fingers along his smooth cheeks into his purple hair and held him still while I softened the kisses from ravenous, devouring ones to light, gentle pecks.

He smelled like a combination of a hundred different products, but underneath it all there was the familiar cinnamon sugar smell he always carried around because of his job at the bakery.

"I swear to god," I mumbled into his mouth. "I could fucking eat you right now."

"Ohmygod I'm gonna jizz my pants," he croaked, bucking his hard-on against one of my thighs. "This isn't happening. I'm dreaming. I think the cat had rabies."

"Not dreaming," I said before kissing across his cheek to nibble his earlobe. "You taste like perfume. And sugar."

"I... I... *oh my god.*"

His legs began to wobble, so I reached down and cupped his ass, pulling him up until his legs automatically wrapped around my waist. "We're going inside. Tell me now if you don't want to."

"Hm?" Stevie's nose nuzzled under my chin, tickling a little.

"Steven, do you want to come inside my house with me?"

"Uh-huh."

My hands kneaded his tight ass cheeks through his skinny jeans, bringing him even closer against me. His cock poked my stomach, distracting the hell out of me. I wanted it in my mouth. I wanted him screaming in pleasure. I wanted him goddamned naked and begging.

"Do you understand what that means? That you're going to take off your clothes for me? Let me touch you?"

"Hm?"

I stopped sucking at his neck long enough to look at him. His pupils were blown, and he looked dazed.

"Sweetheart, I want to get you naked in my bed. I want to bury myself in your body and make you come so hard you pass out. And then I want to keep you here all night so I can do it again and again as often as you'll let me. Do you understand?"

"Huh?"

He was so goddamned cute, kiss-drunk and brain-dead from arousal. I wanted to fuck him so badly, but I wanted to snuggle the shit out of him too. The man was like a drug, and I couldn't get a deep enough toke despite already being very high on him.

I made my way through the front door and into the main room, laying him down on the giant leather sectional sofa and then kneeling beside him to cup his face and make eye contact with him.

"You're so bright and beautiful," I breathed before I could think of what I'd really meant to say.

"I'm dreaming, but please, Chief... please don't wake me up." His eyes were wide and hopeful, a tiny crease of worry between them.

"You're not dreaming, sweetheart. But I don't want to start something if—"

"Shit! The cat! We just left him out there," Stevie said, seeming to shake himself out of his stupor, at least partway.

"Baby, that was a raccoon. It needs to stay outside."

Now his crease of worry turned into a deeper one of confusion. "A raccoon?"

I nodded. "I assume you're talking about the animal Sassy tossed at us before she left?"

"That was my new cat."

"No. That was a wild animal." I wanted to laugh, but I didn't dare risk upsetting him or making him feel stupid in any way. "It had stripes. And a black mask."

"Yeah. I was going to name it Zorro..."

Okay, I couldn't hold back anymore. After sitting on the sofa and pulling him into my lap, I howled with laughter. "You are seriously the most unique, exquisite creature I've ever met, Stevie Devore."

He shifted around until he was straddling me with his arms around my neck. His purple hair, which was currently long on top and shaved on the sides, was messy from my greedy fingers earlier.

"I have to go to work," he said hesitantly. "But... I..."

"I thought you had Thursday afternoons off?" I interrupted.

"No, my other job. The night shift one at the hospital."

My fingers found their way into his hair again. "What hospital job?" I didn't like the idea of him working the night shift *at all*. Bad shit happened overnight. Roads were way more dangerous in the middle of the night. I'd responded to too many grisly accidents to be okay with him on the roads that late at night.

"Why are you frowning?"

"What hospital job?" I repeated.

"I run the coffee cart. Not sure whether you're aware of this or not, but working the front counter at a bakery doesn't exactly keep a girl in high heels and makeup. So I supplement."

His eyes skittered away from mine as he said it, and I realized the second job wasn't for something so frivolous as extra baubles and styling products.

"How much do you need?" I asked.

He began to climb off me, but I wrapped my arms tighter around him until he settled.

"Nothing. It's fine. Things are just extra tight right now since my brother isn't around to help anymore. I have a new job starting this weekend that will cover it anyway."

"Let me help you," I insisted. While we'd been dancing around each other for months, now that I had him here, in my home and in my arms, I wanted to take care of him. I didn't want him to want for anything if it was in my power to give it to him.

"What... what is this, Ch... *Evan*? Why are you being so nice to me? You don't even like me."

I pulled one arm from around his back so I could trace his puffy bottom lip with my thumb. The skin of his jaw was baby smooth, and I wondered if he could even grow a full beard yet. He was so damned young.

"Not true," I said, my voice deeper and rougher than I'd intended. "I do like you. In fact, I like you very, *very* much, Stevie."

His eyes nearly popped out of his head in surprise. "That's not possible. You're... *you*." He gestured to me as if it were obvious. "And I'm... all *this*." He gestured first to the bright yellow sweater set he wore that seemed to be covered in raccoon hairs. Then he indicated his face that could only be described as kiss-roughened and lip-gloss-smeared. He was stunning as usual.

I lifted a brow at him.

Stevie suddenly gasped. "You're drunk! Oh my god," he said, scrambling off me and backing away until he ran into the wall with a squeak. His accusing index finger jabbed at the air. "You're on something. What is it? Should I call an ambulance? Should I call the fire house? I could call Luanne at the sheriff's—"

"Please come back," I said as calmly as I could manage. Seeing him next to the umbrella stand that held walking sticks and a golf umbrella reminded me just how small he was, and that fired up every protective instinct I'd ever had for the young man. "I want to hold you so badly. I've been waiting a long time to touch you, sweetheart. And I'm neither drunk nor high. Come here."

He took a hesitant step closer. "You sure? Because you've never even flirted with me before."

"You're kidding, right?" I slid off the couch and began knee walking toward him. "What do you call my daily visits to Sugar Britches?"

Stevie tried to take a step back again, but the wall was still there. "I call that needing a caffeine fix."

I fell onto my hands and crawled the rest of the way. "I prefer soda."

"You do?" he asked in a whisper, freezing where he stood in utter disbelief.

"Seeing you is what really starts my day and boosts my heart rate," I murmured as I reached him and ran the side of my face up the leg of his jeans. "Not the coffee."

His hands threaded into my hair. "You're like a lumberjack mixed with a silver fox."

"Let me suck you off." I couldn't keep my hands off him. He needed to be naked. His cock needed to be on my tongue and in my throat. Right now.

Stevie was panting, breaths pulling in and out of him quickly. I noticed his hands tremble against my scalp.

"Yes," he breathed. "Please."

5

STEVIE

OHMYGOD. Oh my god. *OH MY FUCKING GOD*.

A whisper in my head that sounded particularly Sassy-like suggested I admit to the status of my virginity before letting Evan in my pants.

Sassy could go to hell.

"Suck me, please," I said again, trying desperately not to sound so desperate.

Evan's large hands were rock steady as he sat up to unfasten my jeans. He had crawled on his hands and knees to me. The man had *crawled on his hands and knees to me*. Can we just... be still and let that sink in for a moment? The man crawled on the floor à la Patrick Swayze in *Dirty Dancing* and gave me That Look. You know the one. The *I'm going to use your body as a penis party hat* look?

I realized he was staring at me with a grin on his face. His eyes were like steely granite and were known to scare the shit out of new recruits at the fire house, but when he smiled like that, it softened his entire face. Everyone referred to the chief as a tough boss and a serious man when he wanted to be, but if they'd ever seen that smile, how could they be intimidated by him? Sassy said he only smiled like that around me, but I knew she was a bullshitter.

Evan was still smiling up at me. What was he waiting for? I whined a little and accidentally thrust my hips forward, which only made his smile more glorious. His fingers reached around to sneak down the back of my pants, slowly pushing the jeans down but leaving the thong in place. I wondered if he realized what he was doing. Who was I kidding? This was Evan Paige. Of course he knew what he was doing.

"Impatient?" he asked.

"Horny," I breathed.

Once my pants were down, Evan finally seemed to realize I still had underwear on. A deep purple comfort thong that had started off as a joke after I began stealing Sassy's jeans. I'd claimed she could have them back if she didn't mind that I'd worn them commando. She'd screeched and said, "At least wear a fucking thong!" Then for Christmas she'd given me an oatmeal canister full of various novelty underwear in front of her entire family. Nico had immediately swiped the pair of boxers with stethoscopes for his husband, West. Otto had grabbed the pair that had fire hoses on it, and I still shuddered every time I thought of Sassy's grandpa grabbing the pink lace thong and sneaking it into Doc's pocket.

I blinked away the mental image of Doc and Grandpa doing the nasty.

Evan must have sensed the slight wilting of my lily.

"You okay? You want me to stop?"

"Are you fucking insane?" I snapped. "Of course I don't want you to stop."

Evan snorted and ran a fingertip under the elastic of the thong, brushing against the crease where my thigh met my sac. That light touch was more than enough to re-juice my banana.

Oh *yes*. "Just like that." Hopefully, I didn't sound quite as breathless and croaky as it seemed. He continued to tease me with light touches at the edges of the tiny underwear and hot breaths against my skin until I couldn't stand it anymore. "JESUS FUCKING CHRIST TAKE THEM OFF ALREADY."

Within three seconds I was buck naked on the floor.

Like, completely, what happened to my sweater set, naked. The chief's intense eyes bore down on me from above, and I felt pinned like a bug under a microscope. "I love it when you're sassy, but don't for a minute lose track of who's in charge here."

A spurt of precum launched out of my dick and onto his chest.

I nodded. "Mm-hm." And then, because, let's be honest, I'm *me*, I added, "Yes, *sir*," in the sexiest purr I could manage.

His gray eyes turned molten, and he lunged for my mouth, sucking and biting and kissing me with such complete ownership, I nearly sobbed with relief and encouragement. My hands shot into his hair and held his face to mine. The coarse texture of his jeans pulled at the tender skin of my inner thighs as he nudged my legs apart with his own. Evan took a final nip at my bottom lip before teasing and sucking his way down my throat to my nipples and beyond. By the time his mouth landed anywhere near my poor penis, I was beyond conscious thought.

"Please, Evan, please... *nnghhh*, god... please oh please... right there... like that... DON'T STOP!"

His big hands were everywhere on my skin when they weren't jacking my dick or caressing my balls. When I wouldn't stop babbling humiliating pleas, he reached up and gently pinned me by my neck, sending my eyeballs back into my head and my brain into a place of complete prickling static. His mouth was a tight grasp on my shaft, and his tongue swirled around it in a wet, sucking torture.

My climax was a city bus barreling down with no concern for the little scared twink in the road. It slammed into me at full force, sending me screaming and scrabbling at Evan's hair, shoulders, and arms as I emptied into his throat. I vaguely noticed him cleaning me afterward with his mouth before gathering me up and moving me to a deep, comfortable bed and sliding in beside me to wrap me in his arms.

Just before drifting off, I heard the low grumble of his confession.

"I've never been with anyone as amazing and responsive as you before."

I thought to myself with a drunken snort, *That's funny, because I've never been with anyone at all before.*

6

EVAN

I HEARD the words he murmured but knew they couldn't possibly be true. While I didn't like it, everyone in town knew Stevie was a voracious flirt. He hit on everyone, and I mean *everyone*. It drove me up the fucking wall. Even before I thought of him that way, seeing him flirt with random people made me stupidly protective. No one was good enough for him. *No one.*

As I lay curled around his smaller body, holding him snugly against my front, I forced myself not to succumb to the desire to drift off and join him in slumber. He'd said he had to work at the hospital that night, and I'd be damned if I was going to be the cause of him losing a job he clearly needed.

Once I was sure his breathing indicated the steady rhythm of sleep, I carefully eased out of the bed and made my way back out to the main room to find my phone. Sassy's number was saved in my contacts list from the time her fire alarm kept misfiring in the old Victorian home where she lived above her brother's medical practice.

I texted her. *What time does Stevie need to be at the hospital?*

A few moments later, her response popped up. *Not until eight. Why? Isn't he still there? You can ask him.*

I responded. *He fell asleep.*

A minute later she replied with a shocked-face emoji. *Wake him up in time to shower and change. His clothes are in the green dragon.*

After thanking her, I set an alarm on my phone as I wandered out to the chest of drawers in the yard. It was quite a sight to behold. In addition to being pea green, it had ivy vines stenciled on the drawers in light pink puffy paint. Someone had done a number on what was most likely quite a high-end piece of woodwork under all that paint garbage.

Instead of trying to manhandle it all the way to my workshop, I went to the garage to grab the hand truck I used to haul lumber and materials. Once the dresser was safely stashed in the workshop, I found Stevie's backpack in one of the drawers and made my way back to the house.

I stripped down to boxer briefs and slid back into bed next to his warm body, pulling him into my chest and wrapping arms and legs around him to get as much of his skin touching mine as possible. He mumbled something that sounded a lot like "dildo drawer" before nuzzling my armpit and settling back down.

Stevie fit against me like he and I had been formed in a mold together. Yes, there was an age difference between us of over twenty years, but there was something about the young man in my arms that felt fated. Purposeful. Meant to be. He was mine. Deep down, I simply knew that to be a fact the same way I knew I'd always been meant to fight fires. It just was.

I kissed the top of his head and murmured to him about how lucky I was to have him there and how I never wanted to let him go. I fell asleep wondering what he needed the money for and what kind of new job he'd been alluding to in order to get it.

When my phone alarm went off, I was surprised to wake up with a warm body against mine. It had been over a year since I'd had the pleasure of waking up next to someone, and I took a moment to simply enjoy it. His cinnamon-sugar-and-floral smell now coated my sheets and pillowcases, making me wonder how long I could go without washing them before it became a health hazard.

"Sweetheart, you need to get ready for work," I said softly before brushing the hair back from his face and resting my lips on his warm forehead. "I put your bag in the bathroom so you can take a shower and get ready here."

"Mpfh." The response was a warm puff of air against my bare chest.

"I'll drop you off and pick you up after. You just need to tell me what time you get off."

Suddenly his brain engaged, and he realized he was in bed with someone he wasn't expecting. He gasped in shock, rearing up and scrambling off the bed backward until he fell on the floor with a painful thump.

"Fuck."

I crawled over to the far edge and peered over. "What happened? Are you okay?"

His stunning crystalline eyes were wide in shock. "God bless America. It really wasn't a dream?"

I'd never seen a more enticing sight than little Stevie Devore naked as a jaybird and sleep rumpled on my bedroom floor.

"I will give you three seconds to get your sweet ass behind that locked bathroom door before I can no longer guarantee allowing you out of this house tonight," I warned in a growl.

The consolation prize for his compliance was the sight of his beautiful bare butt racing across the room.

7

STEVIE

"I'll take one of your delicious hot holes please."

I stared at the customer in line at Sugar Britches. "You did *not* just—"

"Yes, ma'am," Nico cut me off, pushing me behind him toward the kitchen. "Did you want the egg or oatmeal one?"

A *bowl*. Oh shit. She wanted one of our new breakfast bowls. God, what was my problem? Nico had already chewed me out once this morning for giving a customer a large iced tea instead of a small black coffee. The man had stood there blinking between the icy drink cup in his hand and the small coffee cup I'd handed to a preteen girl right next to him (who'd ordered a donut with no drink). Luckily, the customer hadn't had enough caffeine yet to form the words needed to gripe at me about the mistake. Nico simply grabbed the drinks out of both their hands, gave the coffee to the guy, the tea to the older lady far back in the line who must have been a regular, and asked the girl what kind of donut she'd wanted again while nudging me back into the kitchen with his hip.

I couldn't stop thinking about Evan. Getting sucked off by Evan. Receiving fellatio from Chief Paige of the Hobie Fire and Rescue Services brigade. OMG, like, seriously?

Evan Paige gave me head.

I looked around furtively to make sure no one heard my brain squeal that last part. The only other person in the kitchen was Rooster, the tattoo artist Nico had recently hired for the shop upstairs. Well, his name was probably Patrick or something equally boring, but I was convinced he looked more like a Rooster, so that's what I called him.

He lifted an eyebrow at me. "You losing your shit, little buddy?"

I shot him a look for the overly familiar use of a condescending pet name. "Sure am, tiny cock. Why are you down here and not upstairs?"

He stood his giant self up from the poor little wooden stool that had been struggling to hold his weight. The man was eleven thousand feet of leather, ink, and beard hair. His hands went straight for his belt buckle.

"I'll show you a little cock," he muttered.

"Bury your pipe, big daddy. Ain't nobody in here want a piece of that," I snapped back. I was in no mood today. None.

"That's not what you told me last week," he said with a slow grin before taking a seat back on the stool. I was pretty sure I heard it squeak out a whimper of complaint at the burden.

"Last week I was on Vicodin," I reminded him. "And I only said that because I had a broken tooth, and I wanted to see what kind of mark it would make on tender skin."

Rooster chuckled softly under all that beard hair. He was a very laid-back guy, which meant he was mostly quiet compared to the rest of us. "That reminds me. Chelsea told me to tell you she didn't appreciate you hitting on her man."

"You tell that skanky ho I wouldn't touch her man if—"

"What the hell is wrong with you today?" Nico asked in exasperation while chucking an empty tray in the general direction of the sink of dirty dishes. "You are completely off your game. You even asked Sassy if she wanted a pecan bar."

My heart shot into my throat as I gasped. "She's allergic to nuts!"

"I know. That's my point. Your head is in the clouds. Did something happen? Is it the night job? Are you even sleeping at all?"

I thought about my shift the night before. The entire eight hours had been spent with my head in the clouds remembering my time in the fire chief's bed.

In the fire chief's *mouth*.

My dick got hard for the thousandth time in the past twenty-four hours. "I need you to tell me everything you know about sucking cock," I blurted.

The kitchen went completely silent. Even the refrigerator gasped in shock. At least I imagined it did since everyone else in the room had.

"Say what now?" Nico asked at the same time Rooster asked, "Is there a right way?"

I ignored the heat slithering up my neck and pressed on. "Giving head. I need to know all the best tricks. C'mon. Spill."

Nico's jaw had dropped, and Rooster's mouth was in some kind of grin I couldn't quite see beneath the beardy bush.

I rolled my eyes. "Stop with the dramatics."

Nico turned to Rooster. "Did he... did *Stevie* just ask *me* to stop with the dramatics? Is today Opposite Day?"

Rooster snickered. Fuck this, I didn't have time to delay. I had plans to see Evan again the very next day for my stripping lesson. *Paint* stripping. I grabbed a banana, making sure it was the biggest of the bunch. A man had to assume certain things when the object of his lust was large and in charge in both height and muscle mass.

"Here. Show me on this."

"A banana?" Nico asked. "Really?"

"I don't have an eggplant, so do the best you can."

I wandered over to take the stool next to Rooster. The two of us focused on Nico as if he was about to teach us the secret to the universe. And if there was a goddess, he was. Because I'd been avoiding Evan's calls and texts out of sheer terror since he'd dropped me off at work the night before, but there was no way I could avoid the Saturday "stripping lesson" we had planned.

And I wanted to be ready for anything.

Nico frowned. "Why are you even asking me this? Surely you're better at it than I am."

I blinked at him. "Me? I've never sucked anyone off before. How the hell would I know what to do?"

Nico and Rooster howled with laughter. "Yeah, right," Nico said through tears. "You had me going there for a minute."

I felt my jaw tick. "It's true. Stop laughing at me." If I wanted him to teach me the good stuff, I needed to not murder the motherfucker right now. My hands clenched so tightly, the nails dug into my palms.

"Stevie, surely you know your reputation around town?" Rooster asked. "You hook up with everyone. You're Hobie's biggest flirt."

"I may be Hobie's biggest flirt, but I'm not Hobie's biggest ho. It's all for show." My poetry skills were on point, but I kept that knowledge to myself so as not to derail the conversation.

"Wait," Nico said, sobering up from his laugh-athon. "You're saying you haven't really hooked up with all the guys you go out with?"

"I don't kiss and tell," I spat. "That would be rude."

Nico exchanged a glance with Rooster before looking back at me. "But how in the fuck have you been a gay man going out on dates with a ton of different guys and not gotten sexual experience? Are you sure you're not pulling our legs?"

"Am I sure I've never had sex? Why, yes, Nico. I'm pretty sure I'd remember that. I know I've gotten pretty drunk a few times, but from what I've heard, a sore ass might have clued me in the next day had I done something stupid the night before."

Nico held out his hands to calm me down. "You're right. I'm sorry. I'm just really... surprised. That's all. Not even oral? Really?"

This time, I gave him my best eat-shit-and-die look until he sighed.

"Okay. I'll show you a few things, but not in front of Norman."

Who the hell was Norman?

Rooster stood up and ruffled my hair like a jackass before wishing me good luck and wandering up the back stairs to the tattoo shop. Huh.

What followed was a scene I would like to forever scrub from my memory. Let's just say there were plums involved. And an oddly-shaped carrot. And spurts of frosting, which... let's be honest, really shouldn't have been red for the purposes of this demonstration.

But Valentine's Day was coming up, and it was all we had on hand.

AFTER THE FRIDAY lunch rush which was made ten times crazier since Nico had been too busy in the tattoo shop to help in the bakery, I caught wind of an animal emergency brewing in the town square. Charlie's dog, Mama, was missing in action. I spent the better part of an hour helping look for her before we found her curled up in the display window of the antique store down from Charlie's pub. By the time the adoring crowd dispersed, I realized I only had three hours to run home, shower, change, and make it to Dallas for my audition at Feathers.

I made it there with about ten seconds to spare after begging my piece-of-shit Ford Focus to squeeze into a tiny spot between a Suburban and a Hummer in the nearest parking garage to the club. Thank Goddess it was a cool night because otherwise my hair would have defluffed and my dewy complexion would have slid into swampy territory.

Along with a healthy ten-pack of gorgeous hotties, I spent the next four hours learning what it meant to be a Feathers dancer.

Skin. It meant lots and lots of bare skin.

And penises. Those too.

There was no way in hell I could strip off my clothes for cash. I just couldn't do it, especially not if I had any chance of starting a relationship with Evan. But I really needed the money. When the audition wrapped up and Darius pulled me into his office to offer me the job, I gathered up my nerves and asked if there was any way he'd consider hiring me as a bartender instead of a dancer.

His eyes had widened in surprise. "You have experience tending bar?"

"No, sir, but I worked nights as a barback in my town's restaurant until they gave the job to the manager's daughter six months ago. I've memorized all the drinks already and am super friendly." I gave him my flirtiest smile in a way I hoped read more like "I'm a money-earner" and less like "I'll give you head in exchange for a job."

By the time I left there after midnight, I was still officially a dancer for Feathers. Darius had said he'd consider moving me over to work behind the bar, but he'd like me to sleep on it since he'd much rather have me as a dancer. I'd reluctantly agreed because I needed the money either way. I'd also broken a personal rule and allowed myself to be pressured into taking a shot of tequila with the other dancers. Between the shot and the anxiety over managing any kind of late-night job in Dallas when I lived in Valley Cross, my nerves were getting the better of me. I was pretty sure they were lingering around ten gazillion right about now.

So it really shouldn't have come as a surprise when my distraction caused me to miss the fact I was out of gas. I coasted to a stop along the edge of the quiet country road leading from the interstate to Valley Cross. Barren fields stretched out on either side, and at this time of night, there wasn't a single other car anywhere close.

Fuck.

I picked up my phone to call Sassy, mentally kicking myself for getting into this mess in the first place. The poor woman needed her sleep. She had plans to spend the following day on a long trail ride with her niece and two of her sisters.

When my screen lit up though, it was filled with texts and missed calls from Evan with escalating concern about whether or not he'd done something to upset me when we were together on Thursday. My heart tightened in my chest as I saw the last text.

I've clearly misunderstood your feelings, and for that I'm truly sorry. Please be happy and safe.

My jaw ached and eyes stung. I was such a fucking coward, and now he thought I didn't want to be with him.

I clicked on the icon to call him. When he answered, his voice was rough and deep.

"Sweetheart, are you okay?"

"Yeah. I'm okay." I took a deep breath and closed my eyes. "I ran out of gas out by the Lucky Diamond Ranch. Can you come get me?"

The sigh of relief came through the phone and wrapped itself around me. "Of course I can. I'll be there in fifteen minutes. Will you stay on the phone with me until I get there so I can make sure you're okay?"

I smiled at the concern in his voice. "You worried about me, Chief?"

There were a few beats of silence broken only by muffled background noises I assumed included him stomping into boots and grabbing his keys.

"You have no idea," he finally said. "I had to hold myself back from telling you to lock your doors."

I made sure the doors were locked. "Is that your way of telling me to lock my doors?"

The low chuckle sent shivers down my spine. "If you would be so kind. Now tell me why you were in the city so late tonight."

It was pretty clear from my location I'd most likely been coming back from Dallas. Especially on a Friday night, there was nothing else out this way for someone like me other than the lure of the urban clubs and bars. But I'd be damned if I was going to tell him I'd auditioned to shake my wang at a bunch of horny strangers. He'd go ballistic and likely wrap his truck around a tree before he even got off his own property.

"I was dancing at a club," I said instead. Not a lie, really. I didn't want the man to think I'd ever lie to him outright. But I also knew if I told him I'd gotten a job in a city a couple of hours away, he'd piss himself with worry about me on the roads late at night. And that wasn't even taking into consideration how he'd feel if he knew the job included my bare body parts being exposed to a bunch of horny men.

"Who were you with?" he asked. Suddenly, I wanted to laugh because he sounded like he was trying so hard to be nonchalant.

"No one. Just me. I drove down there, danced, and decided to come home early."

I could hear the noise of his truck in the background.

"Baby, it's almost three in the morning," he said softly.

"I know. But I left there around midnight. I just... I didn't pay attention to my gas gauge." I glared at the guilty gauge as if giving it the stink eye would make it suddenly full again.

"Did you have fun dancing?"

I thought back to being the center of the group of dancers in the large practice space above the club. How special and talented I felt just being included.

"Yeah," I admitted. "I really did."

"Good. Maybe next time I could come with you? I'd really love to see you move. I can only imagine all that sexy energy on the dance floor." The rumble of his voice was getting to me, and I reached down to palm myself despite knowing he was getting close. I wasn't sure if I wanted him, or anyone else for that matter, discovering me jacking off on the side of the road. I must have let out some kind of sound because his voice dropped even lower. "Steven?"

"Yes, sir?" I breathed.

"Are you thinking about showing me some of your dance moves?"

I hadn't been, but I was now.

"Uh-huh."

"Will you let me bring you back to my place so I can put some music on?"

Oh dear god.

"Mm-hm." My hand had snuck inside my open pants and was busy stroking my length and fondling my sac. "If you want."

"Oh, I want, sweet darlin'," he said in a deep drawl. "I want more than you can ever imagine. Now get your hand out of your pants and zip up. I'm standing outside your window."

8

EVAN

THE SIGHT of him with his hand down his pants and his head thrown back in pleasure was enough to make me almost swallow my tongue. Fighting my inner caveman, I did my best to hustle him out of his death trap of a vehicle and into my truck without stripping his clothes off and attacking the poor man.

"Thanks for saving me," he said when we were halfway back to my house. I hadn't even asked him if he was okay staying over at my place, because, honestly, I wasn't going to accept a negative answer. So what was the point?

He sounded exhausted. The poor thing had been burning the candle at both ends. Since I'd dropped him off at the hospital for the night shift the night before, I'd learned he was also doing odd jobs at the Wilde Ranch for extra money. Lord only knew when he was getting any sleep.

I reached over and ran my fingers through his hair, preparing to tell him I'd always come when he needed me, when I realized he'd already slumped over and fallen asleep. As soon as I parked the truck in my driveway, I opened the front door and went back to gather the sleeping Stevie into my arms, chuckling to myself at the repeat of tucking him safely into my bed.

Once again, I knew he most likely had to work in only a couple of hours, so I set my phone alarm before stripping both our jeans off. His plain white cotton briefs surprised me. I couldn't imagine they were the sexy underwear a clotheshorse like Stevie would choose for a night on the prowl.

"I'm awake," he mumbled to me at one point while I was undressing him. "Want you."

I snorted softly. "Then take me, big man," I teased in a whisper as I leaned in to remove his shirt. His clothes smelled like male sweat and tequila, which made my nostrils flare with ridiculous amounts of jealousy. I couldn't stand thinking of him in the center of a crowded club dance floor with strangers' hands all over his sweet body. And something about seeing him in just those smooth, cotton briefs made me feel even more protective of him for some reason. I hated the idea of him being taken advantage of by someone charming and slick, especially when Stevie himself had only ever been out of the Texas countryside for brief visits to the city. What if someone slipped something into his drink? What if someone took him back to their place and overpowered him? He was small and still carried a small-town naiveté in some ways.

I thought back to what he'd mumbled the day before about never having been with anyone. Could that be true?

After dropping our clothes onto the chair next to my closet, I snuggled in next to him in the rumpled sheets I'd left behind when he'd called me stranded.

He instinctively turned and curled up against me the same way he had before, and I wrapped my arms tightly around him. This made twice in as many days I'd had Stevie asleep in my bed without being able to take my sweet time worshipping his naked body.

If I was lucky, the third time would be the charm.

One of the shitty things about being over forty is the inability to fall back asleep after you've been woken up in the wee hours of the night.

Sleep evaded me that night, so I simply lay there with Stevie in my arms and enjoyed being in the moment as best I could. When it was finally almost time for my phone alarm to blare, I reached over to turn it off and snuck out of bed to the kitchen.

About six months ago, I'd walked into the bakery in time to overhear Stevie and Sassy joking around about their fantasy boyfriends bringing them breakfast in bed. I forgot what Sassy would have chosen, but Stevie's fantasy had burned itself into my memory.

He wanted cinnamon french toast with lots of real butter and syrup along with extra-crispy bacon, a giant glass of fresh orange juice, and a cloth napkin. Sassy had laughed at the napkin detail, and Stevie's face had lost a little of its sparkle as he'd explained never having had one before. His family's dinette set had a resident roll of dollar-store paper towels that lived in the center of the table. Even paper napkins were something saved for special occasions.

I didn't have a bag of oranges or a juice press, but I had the rest, and by god, he was going to get the star treatment.

When I brought the tray into the bedroom, Stevie was just shuffling back from the bathroom. He must have heard me moving around in the kitchen.

"Hey," I said, suddenly feeling nervous.

"Hey," he said with a shy smile. Stevie's eyes moved from me to the breakfast tray and widened. "What's that?"

"I fixed myself some breakfast," I said, sitting on the bed and propping the tray on my lap. Stevie's eyes dropped to the floor before he looked around for his clothes.

"Oh. Okay. Well I guess I'd better—"

As quickly as I could, I sat the tray on the bedside table and raced over to him, grabbing his shoulders and accidentally startling him. I cupped his jaws and forced him to meet my eyes.

"Stevie, sweetheart, I was joking. I'm sorry I did a piss-poor job of it. I made this for *you*."

A deep blush flooded his cheeks, and his eyes darted away again. Had I embarrassed him? Dammit. I was such a fucking idiot.

I pulled him into my arms. "I'm so sorry, I'm an ass. Will you let me make it up to you and serve you breakfast in bed?"

"I... I should probably go. I have to—"

"Work. I know. And I'm happy to drive you. Whatever you need. Just please... please eat first."

My heart was pounding in my chest with fear that I'd fucked everything up. That I'd scared him off or made him hate me for being a sarcastic jerk.

He leaned back to look at me before tilting up the edges of his lips in a smile. "You made me breakfast in bed? For real?"

I led him back to the bed and got him settled against the headboard before setting the tray on his lap. "Yes. Cinnamon french toast, crispy bacon, orange juice—sorry it's not fresh—and a—"

"Cloth napkin," he said in awe. "How did you know?"

I shrugged. "I listen when you talk. I like what you have to say."

He stared at me. "But I'm a loudmouth."

I thought back to the way his mother had treated him at the scene of the apartment fire when he was a teenager. No doubt that label had come from her or the jackass brother.

"Then I guess I'm attracted to loudmouths." I leaned over and kissed him on the corner of his mouth. "And beautiful mouths." I kissed him again on the other corner. "And expressive men who aren't afraid to be themselves no matter what other people say." This time my kiss landed directly in the center, and I took my time showing his lips exactly how much I loved and respected them.

When I finally pulled back, he was flush-faced and glassy-eyed. Stevie Devore at his most enticing.

"Eat, sweetheart. Don't forget today's the day we start stripping."

His eyes widened before looking away. "Yeah. Stripping. The paint. Are you sure you still..."

"It's up to you. I'd love to spend the day with you after you get off work, and I'm happy to teach you anything you want to know about wood refinishing. But if you just want to hang out and relax, that's fine too. I'm sure you're still exhausted."

I watched him eat the food I'd prepared and got a strange satisfaction from taking care of him. Everything in me wanted to make sure he was well-fed, well-rested, and happy. If he continued working around the clock, not to mention clubbing on his rare night off, he was going to get sick or worse.

"Will you tell me what you're saving money for?" I asked. "I meant what I said about wanting to help." I tried to keep my tone gentle and not pressure him, but I knew him to be a proud, independent person.

His eyes glanced over at me before looking back down at his plate. I thought he was going to ignore the question, but he finally spoke.

"My sister wants to take dance lessons." As soon as the words were out of his mouth, he went back to eating. Despite his shrug, there was no hiding how important this was to him.

"What about your mom? Doesn't she have a decent job? I thought she did accounts for Donny at Valley Cross Cement."

"Got fired when Kade got sent up. Now she works part-time at the vape shop and can't be bothered to look for something better. Don't ask—it's a long and shitty story. Besides, even if she had the money, she wouldn't spend it on something so frivolous."

"Didn't you dance when you were young? I thought you took classes at the dance studio in town."

He stopped eating and stared at me. "That was before my dad took off when there was money to spare. And how the hell did you know that?"

"I swung by the studio with the old fire chief to pick up his granddaughter once. You were there doing some kind of jazz routine. I remember how tiny you looked compared to the young teenage girls in your class. They all treated you like a baby doll," I said with a laugh. "And you had the most adorable scowl on your face because of it. I thought you were going to lash out and take them all down in a giant hissy fit. But as soon as the music came on, you were gone. Escaped into your own world. Like a switch flipped. I always wondered if you'd grow up to be a dancer."

Stevie's jaw tightened and his eyes blinked rapidly like he was upset. What had I said?

"I really need to get to work," he said gruffly. "Thanks for the food."

He put the tray on the dresser as he made his way to the bathroom. The rest of our time together was spent in awkward silence as I drove him to work. By the time I pulled up outside of Sugar Britches, I assumed I'd messed things up so badly, he'd beg off our date that afternoon.

I hopped out of the truck and raced around the hood to open his door for him. "What time do you finish?"

Instead of keeping his distance from me, he leaned his forehead into the center of my chest and let out a deep exhale. "I'm sorry for being moody. I keep trying to get you to see me as an adult, but I keep acting like a child," he said into my shirt.

I wrapped my arms around him and pulled him closer. "I don't want you to be anyone other than who you are. And I know you're not a child. You're a bright and beautiful man who works his ass off and still manages to make other people smile and laugh every single day. Sweetheart, don't you know you're a shining star? You're the sun and the rest of us are lucky enough to get to revolve around your steady glow."

He looked up at me with watery eyes. "Sweet-mouthed motherfucker," he mumbled with a sniffle. "Will you pick me up at noon? Do you want a coffee before you go?"

"I'll be here at quarter till. And no coffee. Just a little sugar." I leaned in and kissed him softly, taking in the early morning taste of him and reveling in the smell of my soap on his skin. He stood on tiptoes to keep the kiss going as I began pulling back.

"Evan?" he asked in a shy, very non-Stevie voice.

"Yes, baby?"

"Do you think... would it really be okay with you if we took a nap this afternoon instead of starting on the green dragon?" His lips curved into a devilish smile, and I realized he wasn't being shy at all. He was playing me. "I gotta be honest. Sassy and I looked for a woodworking ensemble for me to wear in the workshop, and, well, we couldn't find anything that didn't wash me out." He gestured with his palm in a big circle in front of his face. "This body shows better in a birthday suit than a pair of bib overalls."

Stevie shuddered dramatically and turned to sashay into the bakery. I couldn't help but laugh and smack him on the ass before he got out of reach. That cutie could collar me and pull me around on a leash, and I'd consider myself a lucky man.

"You break it, you buy it, Chief," he called over his shoulder. "Oh, and don't forget to hydrate. I have plans for you later, and I don't want you tapping out from old age."

9

STEVIE

THE PLACE WAS HOPPING EVEN by Saturday-morning standards. I'd hoped to work on perfecting a new nut bar I was creating, but there was such a steady flow of customers, it was almost noon before I even had a chance to catch my breath. Otto Wilde came rushing in dressed in his uniform with my car keys in his hand.

"It's gassed up and parked out back. Chief wanted me to make sure you got his messages about the fire."

My stomach dropped. "What fire?" *Please oh please let him be okay.*

Otto reached across the counter and grabbed my hand for a quick squeeze. "No, no. He's fine. But he had to go to Haskell and take over for their fire chief who's been injured along with several of his fire-fighters in a meth lab explosion. He said he'll call you as soon as he can and said to tell you he put his house key on your key ring in case you want to go over there."

At this, Otto's eyes dropped, and I saw a blush on his cheeks. I wasn't sure whose cheeks were redder: his or mine.

"Oh. Okay. Thanks. You, ah... you didn't need to bring my car here though. I could have gotten Sassy to help me later."

Otto looked back up at me with a grin. "She's on an all-day ride. Plus, are you kidding? The chief wouldn't leave until he was done barking orders to all of us about keeping an eye out for you and making sure you were alright."

I pictured big strong Chief Paige instructing the men at the fire house to look after the flirty twink at the bakery. Wonder how that had gone down.

"Thanks," I said. "I guess. I mean, he's going to be okay, right? Just regular work, not... not going back to that meth lab, right?"

Otto reached across again, this time to clap me on the shoulder. "He's going to be just fine. There's nothing left of the meth lab anyway, and most of his work will probably be done at a desk going through lab results with the investigator. But if you can't get ahold of him for any reason, don't hesitate to call me or come find any of us at the fire house. He probably won't be gone more than a week anyway."

A week? Ugh. Just when I was almost ballsy enough to ask him to take my virginity and toss it permanently onto the pile of other crap I'd kept around way too long.

I nodded. "Thanks, Otto. I really appreciate it."

"Anytime. Stay safe, yeah?"

Watching him leave, I realized it was the first time I could remember not lusting after another firefighter in uniform.

I was fucked.

THAT AFTERNOON, I went home to my place. Well, to my mom's place which was where I lived. The same shitty-ass apartment in Valley Cross where I'd lived most of my life. Before Kade got arrested, I'd been on the verge of being able to afford my own place, but now I was the primary wage earner in our little trio. Living with my mom made me feel like a child which was obviously one of my hot buttons. I spent plenty of nights avoiding the situation by staying over at Sassy's place or working overnight at the hospital, but inevitably I'd find myself back there if only to check on my sister, Willow, and make sure everything was okay.

Willow was on the front walkway chatting animatedly with Aria and Ayana, who lived in the apartment building next door to ours and went to the same school Willow did.

"Hey, ladies," I called as I walked around to my trunk to get out the surprise I'd picked up a few days ago. "Special delivery for Willow Dolores Devore," I called out.

Willow's violet eyes narrowed at me. She hated when I used her full name because it was ridiculous. My mother in her temporary grief at being abandoned by my asshole father had poured all of her sadness into naming the precious baby he'd left behind. Weeping Willow and Lady of Sorrows. I did not get my tendency for drama from inside a cereal box. That shit was in my DNA.

The girls sidled over to the car. "What is it?" Ayana asked. "Something from Sugar Britches?"

She loved saying the name of Nico's bakery, and the three girls giggled as if it were a dirty word.

"Well, I brought some cookies home too. But this," I said, pulling the slender box out of a shopping bag, "is the surprise."

Willow took it from me, pulling the end open and sliding out the soft pink ballet slippers. The girls stared at them in awe for a beat before squealing. "Ballet slippers! Ohmygod ohmygod!"

"After next weekend I'll have enough to sign you up for lessons with Miss Sandra at the dance studio."

"Can she be in our class?" Aria asked. Since I was sure there was probably only one class appropriate for first graders at the small-town studio, I agreed.

"That would be great so your big sister and I can share the driving," I told her. "I'll text Dina before I sign up to make sure it's okay with her."

The girls ran off to tell Dina right away as I made my way upstairs to the apartment. When I walked in, my mom poked her head out from the kitchen. She looked just as down as usual.

"Oh, hey, kiddo. It's just you. Thought it was the landlord again."

Before she could turn back around, I called for her to wait. "I'm signing Willow up for dance lessons next week with the Johnson twins. I'll handle the cost and the driving, so you won't have to worry about any of it." I took a breath in hopes I'd caught her on a good day.

She nodded and muttered, "Yeah, fine," before shuffling back into the kitchen.

Yep. Caught her on a good day. At least she was dressed and talking.

I released the breath and made my way back to my bedroom. All of Kade's stuff was still in half the room per my mother's pleas despite the long prison sentence he'd just begun serving. He'd finally done one too many stupid drug deals with the idiots he called friends. Honestly, it had been a relief to see him sent away. My mom had been very young when she'd gotten pregnant with Kade, and the two of them had been more like friends than mother and child in recent years. I'd worried maybe she was at risk for getting caught up in the same shit as Kade. Luckily, it appeared she was smarter than he was because I'd never seen any sign of her using or dealing.

But, she'd adored him. Needless to say, she'd been devastated at the sentencing. It had been like a death to her, and she'd had to come to terms with the massive disappointment he wasn't as perfect as she'd thought. To add insult to injury, her boss at the cement plant was an uptight prick who'd fired her as soon as he discovered she'd been associating with criminals. His implication her own son was a criminal lowlife had crushed her, but she hadn't been able to disagree with his assessment. Which only depressed her more. The only upside was the change in her attitude toward me. For the first time in my life, she seemed to realize I was the "good" son after all. She'd begun offering vague, hesitant apologies here and there which were so awkward, I just wanted her to stop trying. I was grateful for the change in her attitude, but I'd have been more grateful if she'd snapped out of her funk and found another full-time job.

Her losing that income, especially after hiring a lawyer to help Kade, was a blow. At least she'd been able to take over Kade's part-time job at the vape shop when he left, which meant she got out of bed every day and brought in some money again. I was thankful for that regardless of feeling the greater burden of the living expenses on my measly income.

But despite being employed again, she still wasn't herself. She was still a bit withdrawn, moody, distracted, and getting skinnier by the day. Seeing her had brought it all back to the forefront of my mind, and I realized I'd been spending too much time away from home. Willow needed me. Both of them needed me. I knew Dina, Aria, and Ayana had done a great job having Willow spend lots of time with them to distract her from the loss of my brother, but she needed love and attention from me. From family.

"Mama," I called down the hall toward the kitchen. "How about I handle dinner for us tonight? Anything special you want me to make?"

"I don't care. Whatever you and Willow want."

"Are you working tonight?" I asked. There was no response for a full minute.

"No. I quit. That guy's into some shady stuff, Stevie. And I don't have the energy to deal."

I opened my mouth to scream out a million questions including, "How the fuck are we going to pay rent," when I realized she was full-on depressed. She needed help, but I wasn't sure I had enough money to help her get it. I really needed to start that job at Feathers.

I blew out a breath and lay back on my single bed, pulling my phone out to reread some of the messages Evan had sent me that morning.

Is it strange I miss you already?

If you need anything and can't get me, call the fire house.

Don't forget to take a nap, sweetheart.

Did you get your car? Otto was supposed to bring it to you.

And the last one that had come in only moments before:

There's $200 in a yellow coffee mug in the kitchen cabinet. Please take it if you need it.

I'd expected to feel smothered or at the very least annoyed by his parental attitude toward me. But that's now how I felt at all. Never in my entire life had anyone cared enough about me to remind me to get some sleep or to arrange to get my car gassed up and delivered to me. Or offered me money to ease my financial worries. I carried those messages in the deepest recesses of my heart where I begged fate to let them be real and not part of some elaborate scheme to fool me.

Before I could second-guess myself, I sent him a message back.

Is this really real?

10

EVAN

I was in a meeting around the tiny folding table that served as the Haskell FD's conference room when I saw Stevie's text.

Is this really real?

My heart ached for him. I never wanted him second-guessing my feelings for him or thinking he wasn't worthy in every way. My fingers flew over the screen.

More than real. I'd like it to be permanent.

While I would have preferred to give him that sentiment in person so I could judge his reaction, I needed him to know as soon as possible that I was in this. Whatever he wanted of me, he had. Period. I was his for the taking and for as long as he would have me.

I tried my best to focus on the job at hand. The explosion that had sent half the Haskell force to the hospital had been contained before I arrived thanks to the help of volunteers and crews from nearby towns. Since the investigators were following up on the case, I was left reorganizing the shift schedules for the fire department and assessing the remaining resources to make sure the town was covered while the affected firefighters were out of commission.

The following day was Sunday, and I spent most of the morning at the hospital touching base with the Haskell fire chief. The doctors had assured him he'd be able to return to work on Tuesday if he continued resting and following their orders at home for the next forty-eight hours. I was selfishly relieved to hear it. Every cell in my body was craving Stevie, and I felt like if I couldn't touch him again before a few more days passed, I might lose my shit. I'd only just gotten the sweet man before having to leave him behind in Hobie.

We texted back and forth about little things. I'd ask him how work was at the bakery, and he'd tell me the Hobie gossip. He had a crazy suspicion that Hudson Wilde was attracted to his coworker at the pub, which was ridiculous since Hudson was the only straight Wilde man for miles in any direction. He told me about Carrie-Ann Clapper-Fickle's impending divorce and confirmed the town rumor that Leonard Fickle's much younger wife had been sleeping with the even older owner of Ritches Hardware Store. I wondered if she thought he was wealthier or closer to dying than her first husband. Neither were true.

I texted Stevie some sunset pictures my mom had sent me from my parents' cruise in the Caribbean and answered his never-ending questions about my family and what it was like growing up the youngest of four boys. We discovered that while my parents were close to eighty, his mom was in her forties, only a few years older than I was. Stevie had warned me not to freak out, but I'd just laughed.

Sweetheart, you're the one I worry about having a problem with our age difference, not me.

He'd sent back an eye roll emoji and one of a whale. When I'd asked him what the whale was for, he'd replied with an explanation that there was a type of whale that could live over 200 years. His final words hit me straight in the chest.

You need to do the same.

I thought about his youthful energy and wondered whether or not he'd want to become a father one day. The idea of raising children with someone so fun and confident excited me. Any child would be lucky as hell to have Stevie as their dad. He'd be the fun one, sneaking them ice cream and cookies, while I'd be the strict one reminding everyone, including Stevie, when it was time for bed.

"Why you smiling so wide, Chief?" The question had come from a friendly young recruit in the Haskell FD who was busy inspecting some equipment on the department's MICU. "Got a girl back home you're missing?"

"A guy. And yeah, missing him pretty badly," I responded with a grin. The kid's face dropped and nostrils flared. I could tell he wanted to say something but wasn't sure mouthing off at the interim fire chief was the right decision professionally. He was right.

The recruit glanced across the hood of the MICU at his buddy. Since I'd caught his buddy checking out my ass the night before, I was pretty sure the recruit's homophobia wasn't shared. Sure enough, Buddy's eyes were widened in surprised at me, but instead of a disappointed, disgusted surprise, his was a pleased one.

"Truly, Chief? You're gay?" the man asked.

"Bi, actually. But this is my first real boyfriend." I felt the silly line come off my tongue like I was a grade schooler. "He's hot as fuck, so I've been begging your chief to hurry his ass up and heal already," I said with a wink. The man blushed and turned back to his work, carrying a small smile the rest of the day I understood well. When Otto Wilde had come to work for me in Hobie, I'd felt a sense of relief and brotherhood at having a proudly out member of my team. Knowing I wasn't alone in the kind of "don't ask, don't tell" environment of a Texas emergency services department had been encouraging. We'd had a lesbian EMT on our team for ages, but she kept to herself for the most part since the majority of her social life was in nearby Vilene rather than Hobie. If I'd done something to help that man feel more comfortable in his skin here at work, I'd be forever grateful.

On Monday night, I managed to FaceTime with Stevie while he was on a break at the hospital. He was beautiful as ever and practically vibrated with excitement when he answered the call.

"Guess what? I was right! Charlie and Hudson Wilde are doin' it!"

My laugh filled the tiny hotel room around me. "Wow. I can only imagine how Hobie is blowing up right now. Women all over town just fainted in despair."

"Not at all. That's the shitty part. It's a secret. I can't tell anyone." He looked devastated by it.

"Baby, you just told me," I reminded him.

Tiny wrinkles appeared between his sculpted eyebrows. "But you're my person. You don't count."

My thundering heart jammed up into my throat. "I miss you so much," I whispered hoarsely, reaching out for the phone as if I'd be able to feel his full lips under my fingertips.

Stevie's eyes bore into mine. "When are you coming home?"

"Hopefully tomorrow. Do you have to work tomorrow night?"

"No. Unless you consider riding your dick work," he said with a sassy wink.

The flirt. He'd always been like this with other people but rarely with me. I'd never realized before what a mask it was. He was nervous.

"I don't think that's a good idea," I said carefully. "I think we need to talk first."

His face froze—a rictus between flirty and caught out.

"Why? Talk about what?"

"I want to talk about things before we have anal sex, but I don't want to do it over the phone like this."

I could tell I'd hit a hot button. He got squirmy and lost eye contact with me.

"We don't need to talk. I just want to do it. I've been waiting, and—"

"Sweetheart, have you ever had anal sex before?"

His face flushed deep red before looking off to the side at something I couldn't see. I knew he was in a private room with the door closed, so it was more likely his insecurity than a true distraction.

"Maybe you're right. Maybe this isn't the time for this conversation," he said to the wall.

"Will you wait for me at my house tomorrow night?" I asked as gently as I could. I didn't want him to be self-conscious around me, but I knew trying to talk about it more when I wasn't there to reassure him with touches and cuddles wasn't going to be productive.

"Um... yeah, I guess."

He sounded unsure.

"We don't have to have sex or do anything at all when I get there. I just want to see you." I'd intended to reassure him I wanted him as much for himself as anything physical, but his reaction wasn't what I'd expected.

"Yeah, fine. Whatever. I have to get back to work."

The connection cut off before I had a chance to say another word.

Fuck.

11

STEVIE

I DESPISED BEING TREATED like a child. And Chief Condescending Cocksucker was doing it as if he'd taken the class and gotten the certification. *Treating Your Lover Like A Baby 101: How To Cockblock Yourself Without Realizing It.*

The following day found me in a haze of anger. Who knew you could bag a muffin so hard it would shoot straight through the bag and onto the floor? And apparently there was such a thing as frothing a cappuccino too frothily. But it wasn't until I'd told the elderly Hobie librarian to suck it up and take his coffee black like a man that Nico stepped in.

"Mr. Schneider, Stevie here has been having a rough day. Please excuse him. It's obvious his skinny jeans shrank in the dryer and are causing him to—"

"Oh no you didn't," I snapped. "I would never put designer denim in the dryer. You take that back."

Nico reached across me for the jug of cream and a handful of sugar packets. "Here you go," he continued sweetly to the customer. "And let me grab you one of Stevie's pecan bars on the house. I'm sure you'll appreciate biting into his nuts with abandon once you get your hands on them."

I clenched my teeth against the chuckle that wanted to bubble up. No way was I giving that fucker the satisfaction.

When Mr. Schneider finally waddled out of Sugar Britches, Nico sighed. "You know, there's a difference between colorful and bitchy. Colorful Stevie brings in business like gangbusters. Bitchy Stevie is going to get me killed one of these days."

"Pfft. That man is five feet zero and weighs a thousand pounds. All you have to do is be faster than him."

He lifted an eyebrow at me. "He carries a Glock 42 in an ankle holster."

I felt my bladder clench. "Fuck."

"Yeah, no shit. Texans, am I right?"

We shared a shudder before going back to our work noticeably more subdued. I wondered if Evan carried a weapon. Despite being anti-gun, I had to admit the thought of Evan carrying a weapon was sexy as hell. My dick spent the rest of the afternoon hard as diamonds even though my brain was pissed at the man for treating me like a virgin dweeb. Never mind the fact I *was* a virgin dweeb.

When we finally closed the shop late that afternoon, I'd ramped myself up into a frenzy to the point that when Sassy stopped me in the parking lot to dish some more about that hobag Carrie-Ann and the jackass who owned the hardware store, I snapped at her.

"Nobody gives a shit about the Clapper-Fuckles, Sassy!"

She clicked her teeth closed before muttering, "Clapper-Fickle. And what the hell's your problem?"

"I've been cockblocked by my own virginity," I hissed. "That's my problem. A classic cold case of blue balls."

She whipped her head around and gawped at me, her high ponytail flying around in a dark arc. "What? I thought for sure you and the chief..."

"You'd be wrong."

"What the fuck? Why not?"

I shrugged. "I guess I'm not experienced enough for him. Or maybe it's the opposite. Maybe he's believed all the rumors and thinks I'm a slutty, disease-ridden—"

"Dude, seriously? Calm your shit down. You're about to ignite."

The word conjured up raging infernos with Evan Paige in the center, losing the battle against the blaze. I deflated.

"I'm not good enough for him," I admitted in a small voice. "He's a big strong hero type, and I'm just... a coffee boy."

"Bullshit," Sassy barked, scaring me so badly I jumped. "You are the most amazing person in the world, Stevie Devore. You're adorable and snarky and fun and brave. You're sweet and loving and kind and protective. Who makes sure Willow has milk for her cereal every morning? Who started opening the bakery after Rox moved away just so Nico can have more time with West and Pippa in the mornings? Who saved me the night Terry Jackman got drunk and tried to make out with me?"

I growled under my breath. That guy was a royal skank.

"Right," Sassy said. "You did. Not one of my six brothers or three badass sisters, but little Stevie Devore with his shaved head and Doc Martens."

I remembered that night. It had been at a town bonfire, and I'd been desperately flirting with Nico at the time. After he and West had left in a dense fog of sexual tension, I'd realized Sassy hadn't come back from her trip to the bushes for a pee break. When I'd found Terry grabbing her by a wrist, I'd kicked him in the balls, grabbed my bestie, and raced us both back to the safety of the bonfire.

"That was during my bad-boy phase. I can't believe you let me wear Doc Martens," I whined. "What kind of friend are you?"

"Don't change the subject. Why you no sex up big hunky chief?"

"He doesn't want me."

"Once again, I call bullshit. What's the real reason?"

"I think he's scared of my V card," I admitted. "He wants to talk first."

"Why is that a problem? I think it's sweet."

I hated her. "Listen, high pony, while you sit around swooning over sweetness, I'd like to get laid. I've fucking waited a long fucking time for the fucking, and I fucking plan on fucking, motherfucker."

She blinked at me. "You don't like the ponytail?"

I held a hand up to her face. "I can't even with this. I gotta go."

As I walked swiftly to my car, I heard her call out, "I heard Evan's back in town. You going over there tonight?"

Instead of answering, I shot her the bird. Hell no, I wasn't going over there tonight. If I did, I'd only make a giant fool of myself by begging and throwing myself at him. Or worse, blurting out my increasing anxiety about the Feathers job, which would undoubtably piss him off even more.

No. No going to Chief Sexy Dick's house. A girl's gotta have more dignity than that.

Right?

On my way home, I called Darius at the club.

"Any way you need me to work tonight? I don't care what you have for me. I'll do anything."

12

EVAN

I ONLY HAD the patience to wait for one full hour before I broke and texted him.

Sweetheart, where are you?

No response. I tried calling. No answer. After another thirty minutes, I hopped in the truck and made my way to Sugar Britches, wondering if he'd stayed late to work on a cake or something. But the bakery was closed up for the night, and when I found one of the guys who worked at the tattoo shop upstairs, he said Stevie had left two hours earlier.

Maybe I shouldn't have assumed he'd come straight from work. But he'd agreed, hadn't he?

I texted Sassy to ask if she'd seen him, but her response didn't help.

He's being weird. It's not you, it's him.

I read the text again before responding.

What does that mean? Where is he?

My phone rang.

"Sassy, just tell me if he's okay," I said before she could say a word.

"He's fine. Just a moody bastard," she grumbled. "He's upset because he thinks you're put off by his lack of experience."

My stomach fell. I needed to find him and make sure he knew how crazy that was.

"Where is he?"

"I don't know. Honestly, I hoped he was headed to your place."

"Any other ideas besides his apartment?"

"Well, Hudson's in Dallas, so maybe Stevie went to the pub to keep Charlie company?"

I felt my jaw tighten. Hobie was a small town. I already knew Charlie and Stevie had been out on a date. Even though Stevie had told me Charlie and Hudson were together, I knew what a flirt Stevie was. And if he was mad at me, I could see him turning his flirt factor up to a thousand to get back at me.

If he was with Charlie, I was going to have to rein in my jealousy since I didn't own the poor man. I thanked Sassy and made my way to the unfinished pub, which turned out to be just as dark and empty as Sugar Britches.

I was torn between having to admit he was avoiding me and continuing to look for him like a deranged stalker. What if he just wasn't that into me?

Twenty minutes later I pulled up outside of his apartment. My compromise with myself was checking one more place only. Not the Wilde Ranch. Not the hospital coffee cart. Just his home. If he wasn't there, I'd acknowledge defeat and go home.

I strode up the stairs and knocked on the door. No answer. I knocked again. This time a little girl came up to me from the stairs to the parking lot.

"Mrs. Jodi isn't here," she said. "I'm not apposed to tell you that, but you're a firefighter right?"

I looked down at my uniform. "Yes, ma'am. Do you know if Stevie is home?"

She shook her head, braids with little pink plastic clips on the end bounced around her. "No, sir. He went to Dallas for work. Mrs. Jodi was here, but Willow said she left after he did."

I ignored the comment about Dallas, assuming it was a misunderstanding, and thought of Stevie's little sister, who couldn't be more than six or seven. "Is Willow home alone?"

The little girl shrugged. "That's what she said. My sister said as how she needs to come be with us for supper so's she's not all by herself."

She turned and banged her tiny fist on the door, calling out for Willow. Finally, the door opened a smidge on the chain and a tiny nose peeked out, followed by a pair of eyes the same light purple as Stevie's. They widened when she recognized me from the times I'd seen her at the bakery.

"Chief Paige," she cried with a grin, pulling the door open hard only to have it bounce closed again when it hit the end of the chain. We heard the rattle of the chain before she threw the door open again. "Is something on fire?"

I knelt down to her level so I didn't loom over her. "No, sweetie. I came by to say hi to Stevie, but your friend here said he's at work."

She nodded. "Yeah. He said he has to go to his job in Dallas and won't be home till very late. Past my bedtime. Mama said I have to watch the clock and go to bed when it has a nine and two zeros."

Dammit. I was a mandatory reporter in the state of Texas. If I suspected child neglect, I was legally bound to report it within forty-eight hours. But if I reported his family to Child Protective Services, Stevie would most likely hate me.

What would he want me to do?

"Willow, do you know the name of the shop where your mama works?"

"The Snake Snake?" she asked. "I think?"

There was a shop attached to a local gas station called the Vape Snake. I pulled out my phone to find their number. Before dialing it, I tried Stevie one last time and left him a voicemail.

"Hi, sweetheart. Listen, I know you're upset at me, and I'm sorry, but I'm not calling about that. I'm at the apartment, and Willow is home alone. I want to find out what you want me to do besides try to get a hold of your mom."

After I hung up, I texted him the same basic message and then texted Sassy what was going on in case he'd answer a call from her instead.

Then I called the Vape Snake and discovered she no longer worked there.

I was still staring at the phone when it rang again.

"Chief Paige," I said out of habit.

"He's not answering," Sassy said. "I don't know where he is."

"Willow said he has a job in the city?"

There were several beats of silence. "Oh shit."

"What is it?"

"I'll come stay with Willow."

"Sassy, where is he in Dallas? What's the job?"

"No way. I'm not getting in the middle of this. Best friend trumps fire chief every time."

"Do I need to remind you I'm also your brother's boss?" I growled. Now I was really concerned about Stevie, and it wasn't just his family situation.

"Like I give a shit about Otto's job. Hell, I'd rather him not walk into any more burning buildings if you want to know the truth. Go ahead, fire him."

Fuck.

"Sassy—"

"Gimme twenty minutes, Chief. See you soon."

I hung out on the landing outside the apartment with the girls. At one point another girl who was a carbon copy of Willow's friend joined us with a shoebox of sidewalk chalk. The girls made themselves comfortable drawing pictures of rainbows all over the cement around the apartment door until Sassy pulled up all cheerful and fun like Mary Fucking Poppins.

"Sassy—" I tried again.

"Sorry, Chief! I have to get this sweetie fed and tucked into some homework. Girls," she said, turning to the twins, "your momma's probably expecting you home. G'night everyone!" She hustled Willow into the apartment before shutting the door in my face.

It wasn't until I was halfway back to Hobie I realized it was unlikely a first grader was inundated with homework. Sassy was just as devious as her missing bestie.

By the time morning rolled around, I was sleep-deprived and desperate. There was still no answer from Stevie, and Sassy was a locked vault who kept reassuring me everything was fine. It wasn't fine. I was sick with worry, exhausted after tossing and turning, and distraught from missing the sweet man I'd thought only a week ago might actually be the one.

Regardless of how fucked-up I was, I had to make an appearance at work. I hadn't been to the fire house since the previous week, and my guys needed to see my face. Halfway through the day, I overheard someone mention seeing Stevie at Sugar Britches that morning.

Knowing he was only blocks away and hadn't had the common courtesy to call me to reassure me he was okay broke my heart. And honestly, I didn't have the stomach to go confront him, especially while he was at work.

Finally, later in the afternoon, I agreed to go for a drink with Otto and the sheriff. They wanted to stop by and check on the progress of Hudson's pub on the way to the Pinecone, so I followed them in my quiet funk.

It wasn't until I was inside the Fig and Bramble pub that I heard Stevie's voice from somewhere behind the bar.

13

STEVIE

As I'd pulled up to Feathers the night before, I realized I'd whipped myself into a regretful tizzy over the whole Chief Paige thing. It hadn't been fair of me to assume his feelings about my virginity. That had been so stupid and immature. Not long into the drive, I'd realized how much I'd let my insecurities take over. Evan had made it clear in many ways he was interested in me despite our age difference, and he'd even mentioned wanting this thing between us to be permanent. So when I'd gotten into the club and discovered Darius needed me as a dancer, it had made my misery complete.

Rather than succumb to a horrible case of the pukes, I'd poked my head into Darius's office to ask if there was any way I could keep my boy shorts on or if it was a requirement to strip completely down.

He'd glanced up at me. "As long as you're playing the sexy tease, I don't give a shit. It's your loss at the end of the night when the tips aren't as big." He'd gone back to whatever it was he'd been doing, having no idea how relieved he'd made me.

The night had turned out to be fun as long as I'd been able to stay out of the danger zone, which was approximately the length of the tallest man's wingspan from the dance floor. I'd actually loved dancing and moving, and that night hadn't had any special choreographed numbers I'd needed to worry about. I'd finished up with tons of cash in my wallet and a bit more confidence than I was used to.

Being desired and pursued by all those men, even if it'd only been for purely physical reasons, had bolstered my self-esteem. It had reminded me I was desirable. If the worst case happened and Evan dropped me like a hot potato, there might be other guys out there who'd want me. And honestly, the money was no joke. It had taken some stress off me and then some. I knew I could cover the rent on my own if my mom didn't get her act together. It would be tight, but I could do it.

When I'd arrived home to Sassy's sleeping form on my mom's sofa, everything had gone to shit. She'd told me about Evan's phone call, about my mom leaving Willow home alone, and about Willow letting slip to her that my mother had been visited by "the apartment man" who was mad about "some money."

After waking up this morning, I noticed Mom still hadn't come home, and she sure as hell still wasn't answering the phone. I found an overdue notice in a stack of bills and papers on the kitchen counter and wondered what the hell Mom had done with the rent money I'd given her two weeks before. Obviously, she hadn't paid rent with it.

I'd had to call in late to the bakery so I could get Willow on the bus to school. Thankfully, Dina had offered to keep Willow after school since Aria and Ayana were having a midweek sleepover birthday celebration that night. Willow and I had gone to Save-Mart on Saturday afternoon to pick out cool hair paint and glitter nail polish for the girls' gifts and had painstakingly wrapped them in empty toilet paper rolls and cereal boxes to make it "mysterious" according to Willow's specifications.

Once Willow was off to school and I took my checkbook and the cash from my tips the night before to the landlord's office, I heaved a sigh of frustration and hopped in my car. How the hell was I supposed to face Evan after all of this? He had to think I was trash. If he hadn't already thought it by the way I was going hot and cold on him, he surely thought it now after finding my baby sister abandoned by both my mom and me. And if that didn't do it, he'd sure as hell lose respect for me when I couldn't even afford gas in order to get to work anymore.

I couldn't face him. If there was a goddess, she would keep him out of the bakery all day. One look at him and I might break. It was all too much. My life was a fucking roller coaster of ups and downs. I was a hot mess, and he deserved better.

The bakery was thankfully slammed, and I ended my shift by delivering some treats to Charlie and Hudson at the pub.

They were so stinking cute together, it made me bubble with jealousy. I wanted that. I wanted open affection and someone to touch me the way Hudson did with Charlie. Hell, the guy hadn't even been into men before, and now he was as handsy as could be in front of anyone and everyone. He liked Charlie *that* much.

I swallowed past a lump in my throat as one of the local busybodies started sniffing up Hudson's tree, much to Charlie's amusement and Hudson's squirmy discomfort.

It wasn't until I heard Otto and Sheriff Walker come in that I realized Evan was right behind them.

"Eeep," I cried, diving over the pub's new custom bar top and landing in a ball next to Charlie's feet. "I'm not here," I squeaked.

Augie came into the pub next, informing us Mama was in his antique shop again.

"And I've noticed she looks a little... pregnant," Augie said. "It's not possible Milo..."

Hudson leaned over and whispered to Charlie. "Isn't Milo a cat?"

Charlie's smile was devious. "Should I pull a Stevie and screech to the heavens about someone deflowering my special girl?" he asked.

"Not fair," I whined, feeling awful all over again. "I was beside myself with guilt. I'm going to be the father of a passel of ugly-ass bastards. *Me.* I'm too young and pretty to be a baby daddy."

I heard Evan's deep, sexy voice over the crowd. "Is that Stevie? Sweetheart, get out here, we need to talk."

Uh-oh.

"I'm not here," I repeated to Charlie and Hudson in a frantic hiss.

"Baby, I'm looking right at you," Evan said gently, peeking over the bar top. "C'mere."

The wrinkles of concern marring his forehead as he searched my eyes were the last straw.

"Evan?" I asked, my voice wobbling more than I expected.

"Fuck this," he muttered. Then the big strong fire chief vaulted over the bar, grabbed me up in a fireman's carry, and hotfooted it out the door of the pub before I could take my next breath.

14

———————

EVAN

I KEPT my eyes focused on the road as the truck made its own way home. Stevie's entire body was curled in on itself and crowding against the door to get as far away from me as he could. Every now and then on the short drive to my house I heard a sniffle come from his direction, but I didn't dare reach over to him and risk opening my own floodgates.

Because seeing him hide from me had brought it all in focus. I'd fucked up. Something I had done had intimidated him, scared him, or just plain disgusted him, and now he obviously didn't trust me to even help him as a friend. Honestly, I was surprised he'd even let me put him in my truck. I'd asked him when I got to the parking spot if he'd consent to come to my place so we could talk. He'd said yes in a small voice before climbing into the truck and securing his own seat belt.

He looked so tiny in the cab of the huge truck. I wanted to pull him closer to me and tuck him up tightly against my side. But I couldn't start anything with him until we were alone with time and space to hash things out.

I pulled up in front of the house and hustled over to open his door. Stevie was ready. As soon as the door opened, he launched himself at me, wrapping his arms and legs around me and holding on for dear life.

"Please don't hate me," he said in a watery voice. "I couldn't stand it if you hated me."

I held him as tightly as I could without squashing the poor man and buried my face in his neck.

"I couldn't even if I wanted to," I said gruffly into the warm skin that smelled like cinnamon, sugar, and styling products. "You didn't do anything wrong. I'm sorry I scared you away. Don't you know by now how much I..." I swallowed, wanting to say the words so badly but still afraid of scaring him. "Don't you know by now how much I adore you and want to be with you?"

Stevie's whole body trembled in my arms. "I fucked up, Evan."

"Well, then, it's a good thing you have a partner who does the same and who'll do anything to fix it for you, now isn't it?" I lifted my head up to be able to see as I carried him into the house. I didn't even bother stopping in the living room. Instead, I took him into my bedroom, where I noticed the bed was made up nicely even though I'd left it a jumbled mess. "Did you make my bed, sweetheart?"

He kept his head down on my chest. "Yeah. I slept here the other night. You said I could."

I laid him down gently in the center of the big bed and began removing his shoes and socks. He kept his eyes closed as if afraid to make eye contact with me. "Stevie, thinking of you sleeping here in my bed while I was gone... I wish I'd known. I want you here every night."

He nodded but didn't say anything else. I kicked off my own shoes, emptied my pockets, and climbed up next to him, lying on my side facing him so I could smooth the hair from his face.

"Look at me," I whispered. "Please don't hide your beautiful eyes from me, Stevie."

When he opened them, they were on the verge of overflowing. "Why do you put up with me? I'm a hot mess."

I leaned in to sip the tears as they slid out. "Baby, you were born a hot mess. Did it ever occur to you that's part of what I find incredibly attractive about you? You're fun and flirty, bright and happy. You are never boring and always filled with surprises. Being with you is like opening a new gift every single day. I knew you were a hot mess before I fell for you. But I worry I'm too bossy and overprotective for you. I don't want to dull your sparkle. It would crush me if I were ever the cause of your unhappiness."

His hand came up to caress my face, and I finally saw the beginnings of a smile. "What if I like being bossed around and protected by a big strong fire chief?"

I couldn't wait any longer. I leaned in to take his mouth in mine. He tasted both salty and sweet, the perfect combination. The kisses began slow and tender but escalated quickly as soon as our bodies remembered how fucking badly they wanted each other. Within a few short moments we were panting and grinding, fingers grabbing on to hair and zippers painful against hard cocks.

"Please," Stevie begged. "Please make love to me without a big conversation. I want you. That's enough. Please, Evan."

Something about the way he worded it made the puzzle pieces click together until I finally understood. Stevie wasn't a child, and he needed me not to treat him like one especially when it came to sex. He deserved my respect. And a man respects another man to make the decision that's right for him and reach out for help if needed. He hadn't reached out for help.

I was an idiot.

"I'm sorry," I murmured against his mouth. "I only ever wanted to make sure you were okay. I never meant to—"

His mouth opened in a grin and his eyes shone. "I know. You thought you were looking out for me. But thank you for listening to me now. I'm ready. I'm past ready. And I want you so badly I think I might come in my jock."

The word "jock" set off a nuclear reaction in my nuts. I ripped off his pants to reveal a neon yellow jock with electric-blue rotary telephones on them. Where the hell did he find such insane undergarments?

His slender legs were curved with muscle, and I ran my nose up the inside of a thigh to bury it in the front of his jock.

"Holy fuck, you are so damned sexy," I said, inhaling him. "I swear to god, no one has ever turned me on as much as you do."

"Even a woman?"

I stopped what I was doing and crawled over him to press our foreheads together. When our eyes met, he must have seen the intensity in my gaze. I was getting ready to lay down some truth for him so he'd never doubt my affection again, but before I could speak, he rushed to cut me off.

"Never mind. That was stupid and insensitive. I'm sorry."

"You need to know that I find you more attractive than *anyone*. Male, female, real, imaginary. Anyone."

Stevie's legs wrapped around my hips, and he arched his cock up into my belly. I wanted him desperately, but I wasn't going to continue undressing him until we were clear on this topic. It was important. I'd dated plenty of people in the past who didn't quite understand what it meant to be bisexual. I couldn't afford for Stevie to be one of them.

"I know. I do," he said. "It was just a moment of insecurity. I'm..." He sighed. "There are going to be moments of insecurity, Evan. You're so much more experienced and together than I am, and sometimes I feel like..."

I waited for him to think of what he wanted to say.

"Sometimes I second-guess why someone like you would want to be with someone like me."

I relaxed into him and grinned. "God, that's the easiest thing in the world. I told you already, but I'll tell you again as many times as you need to hear it to believe me. You're sweet and fun and kind. You're loyal and dedicated. Do you know that you make funny nicknames for people? And you'll stop whatever you're doing to help someone carry something heavy even though you're a tiny little thing. You also sing like an angel, but never when you think other people can hear you. And you talk back to yourself in public, which is totally entertaining even though, or maybe especially because, you have a potty mouth. You also do this hip-shimmy thing to get your car door to close right on rainy days. And when you talk about your baby sister, your mouth automatically widens in a gorgeous grin."

I opened my mouth to add to the list of what made him so damned special, but he grabbed me by the face and pulled me in for a deep kiss instead.

I guessed he got the message.

I was crazy for the man.

15

STEVIE

I TRIED DESPERATELY to remember the details of Cinderella's fairy godmother's rules for when shit turned bad. Because the rate I was going with the fire chief, I was about two pumpkins and an eggplant past midnight, and I was not willing to chance losing my shot at feeling the man's foot slide into my glass slipper.

Stop, Stevie. You have no business trying to make metaphors work right.

I squirmed underneath Evan's hard bulk. "As much as I could let you keep talking all night—and believe me we're coming back to your list because it's pretty epic—I really want you to get naked right now," I said over the sound of my heart hammering in my ears.

Evan's lips began a trail of *ohdeargod* down my neck and across my suddenly bare chest. I felt the head of my dick poke out of the top of the cheap jock, leaving a trail of slickness in its wake. My head was dizzy with need and want and confusion over where to put my hands, my mouth, my eyes. It was all so very stimulating and overwhelming. I arched up into him again wanting to talk dirty to him and show him I was an equal partner in our intimacy. But all that came out of my mouth was the word *please*, whimpered over and over in a hoarse chant as my eyes rolled back in pleasure.

His mouth was on me, his hands were all over my skin, and his deep rumbles of satisfaction vibrated throughout my entire body.

"Evan," I begged.

He rolled me over and straddled the back of my thighs, intent on squeezing my ass and fondling the straps of the jock against my cheeks.

"Holy fuck," he breathed, running his fingers under the elastic. "I almost don't want to take this off you."

"Take it off. Please take it off. My dick... I need..." I humped the mattress for friction which seemed to do something to my ass that made Evan's rumbles turn into growls. I felt a finger brush down my crease and across my hole. "Oh god. Oh god," I breathed, squeezing closed against the pad of his finger out of instinct.

"Stay here," he commanded. As if I was suddenly going to run out to the Sip and Save for a pack of gum.

I closed my eyes and counted to ten thousand. Okay, fine. I counted to four before I blurted, "For the love of goddess what is taking you so long?"

Before I finished the last word, there was a slick finger against the entrance to my ass, and I sucked in a breath, trying and failing not to clench.

Evan stretched out on top of my body, his lips sliding along the nape of my neck until they rested against the shell of my ear. His finger gently pressed circles around my hole as he murmured into my ear with that sexy voice.

"Relax, sweetheart. I'm not going to do anything to hurt you. If you want to stop, just say stop."

"I do not want to stop," I bit out through gritted teeth. "If you stop, I'll throw a hissy fit unlike anyth—"

The finger went in, stealing my breath at the same time his teeth bit down softly on my earlobe. Evan murmured something soothing through his busy mouth, but I couldn't make it out. I was too busy carrying around a mental parade banner that said "For A Good Time, Gimme Your Digits."

He toyed with my ass, fingering the hell out of me while I begged and pleaded for more. After he barely grazed my prostate, I propped myself up on all fours and arched my ass back toward him in hopes of getting him deeper, feeling him press against that magical spot again.

"I'm ready," I hissed at one point.

"You're not."

Just as I was preparing to scream at him that he didn't know my body as well as I did, he pushed a second finger in.

Holy ham on a biscuit, that's tight. Maybe he was right and I was wrong, but I sure as hell would never tell him that.

"Oh godddd," I repeated. "Touch my spot. Do it."

"Bossy bottom," Evan said with a chuckle before swiping firmly down against my gland.

Stars shot through the edges of my vision, my balls drew up tighter than ever before, and my dick dropped a thick stream of precum toward the bedcover.

"Newborn baby Jesus, that's incredible," I said in awe when I caught my breath. "I've been dildo-ing wrong all this time."

"No more," Evan grumbled.

"Huh?" I gasped as a third thick finger pierced me.

"You want something inside this precious ass, you come find me. Understand?"

"Nnhhngh."

He stretched me as my brain whirled and my skin prickled. Somewhere in the back of my head I realized I wasn't giving his body any attention, but I couldn't bring myself to do anything other than receive his ministrations. My face was smashed into the comforter, and my arms were stretched above my head to the wooden head-board. I realized it was only my ass still propped up in the air like a wanton hussy.

I fucking loved being a wanton hussy.

"More," I demanded into the smooth fabric of the bedding. The crinkle of a condom wrapper accompanied the squelch of more lube, and I realized he really was going to leave my jockstrap on. My poor penis. It wanted out, but I couldn't move my arms. It was like my entire body was a tuning fork and I didn't want to fuck up the rhythm of the vibrations.

"Turn over, sweetheart. I want to look at you."

Mother of pearl, I was going to cry like a baby. I was going to turn over and sob my undying love to the man and ruin everything.

"Stevie, turn over. I need to be able to see you're okay when I finally get inside you."

His large hand tugged on my hip, pulling me around until I was lying on my back. Evan looked down at me like a damned god from an ancient Greek myth. Strong, square-jawed, and staring at me with full-on intensity.

"This feels good," I said stupidly. "Everything... I mean... yeah. It's good. I'm good."

His face softened into a sweet smile. "I'm glad. It's supposed to be good. Supposed to be great, in fact."

I nodded like an enthusiastic puppy. "Yeah, I know. And it *sooo* is. Like, really good."

Was I allowed to facepalm during sex?

Evan winked at me before working my jock off. Thank fuck, my cock was free. It slapped against my stomach, leaving another string of precum along the skin of my stomach. Evan must have noticed it also, because he leaned down and took a swipe at it with his tongue before swallowing my cock.

Just as I was about to drown him in jizz, he pulled off and grinned up at me with a mischievous look on his face. "Not yet, baby. Not till I'm all the way inside you."

"THEN FUCKING GET UP HERE AND FUCK ME ALREADY FOR FUCK'S SAKE!"

We stared at each other in the ensuing silence.

"You really are being a tease," I said more calmly despite my rapid panting. "My dick is going to explode. Look at it."

We both looked down to the angry, wet, purple prick hopping between us. "Help me," I whimpered. "Have mercy on me, Chief."

His eyes darkened at the title, and he grabbed my knees, folding them up toward my shoulders until my ass was laid out before him like a tasty treat. As he finally, finally pressed the head of his cock against my opening, I met his eyes.

And knew in that moment, I was owned completely by the man on top of me.

16

EVAN

HE WAS STUNNING. By far the most receptive and responsive person I'd ever had in my bed. Stevie was vivacious, sexy, funny, and enthusiastic. With a healthy dose of bossiness sprinkled in.

I already adored him outside the bedroom, but inside? Inside he was everything that was fun and hot about being intimate with another person. Not to mention his body was divine. He was pale and smooth, slender and full of vibrating energy. Stevie Devore was not only edible, he was flexible and snack-sized, which meant I could manhandle him exactly how I wanted to.

And there were a million ways I wanted to.

His eyes were completely glazed over as I pushed into him slowly. I leaned in to kiss him, keeping my weight on my hands and knees. His lips were full and warm, and kissing him was the best thing ever. I nibbled a little bit on his bottom lip and felt him humming his approval as I continued to taste him.

Once I was halfway inside him, I moved my arms underneath his to grasp his shoulders. His eyes were so beautiful—violet flowers that looked at me like I was everything to him. I wanted desperately to be everything to him. I couldn't hold it back any longer.

"I love you, Stevie," I whispered. "I love you."

His eyes widened as my words sunk in. I continued murmuring words of affection as I worked my way in and out of his body until I was fully seated. While I waited a beat to let him adjust to the fullness, I kissed him again and noticed a tear slide down toward his ear.

"You okay, baby?" I asked.

"It's too good to be true," he said, almost too quietly for me to hear. "Did you mean what you said? Or is it just because we're—"

I leaned in to kiss him again before he could say it. "No. No, sweetheart. I said it because I meant it. I've felt this way about you for a while but didn't want to scare you off."

He shook his head, dislodging a few more tears. "You wouldn't. You didn't. Because... because I love you too."

Stevie looked so vulnerable in that moment—creases of worry on his forehead and flicks of his wet eyes away from mine—I thrust my hips in and out to get his attention. His eyes blinked at me in surprise.

"Hey. It's just you and me here. And we love each other." I grinned. "There is nothing to be afraid of. Just fun and love. You and me. All right?"

His face broke out into a smile. "Who knew you were such a talker in the sack? Get a move on, old man. Before you lose your erection and need a little blue pill."

My jaw dropped open before I came to my senses enough to show him just how healthy my erection was and just how much I did *not* need a little blue pill.

"Nnnhhhh!" he cried out as I thrust into him. "Yes. Yes, *please*."

I watched as he threw his head back in pleasure. Maybe our little conversation had given his body enough time to stretch, or maybe it was the ten vats of lube I'd used, but he clearly wasn't experiencing any pain right now. Not if his whimpers for more were any indication.

His body was a tight, hot squeeze around me that caused me to grit my teeth to keep from shooting right away. As I pulled out, his body tugged me back in, and when I pushed back in, I wanted to stay there forever, joined with him as closely as possible.

I moved my hand down to stroke his hard cock, using the copious fluid around the head to slick the way.

"Mpfh," he grunted when I began to jack him. "Mm-hm. Mm-*hmmm*."

His throat was exposed as he stretched his head back. I licked up the side of it and grazed my teeth along his earlobe before sucking it into my mouth.

"Evan," he panted. "Gonna come. *Evan!*"

I let go of his ear with a deep chuckle. "Come for me, sweetheart. Want you to feel good."

His cock pulsed in my palm, which made my own climax creep along my spine. When he screamed his release, I shot hard and deep inside of him, feeling the electric current zing through my lower body in the most delicious way.

Stevie's arms and legs were wrapped tightly around me, clinging for dear life. I dropped light kisses all over his face until he came back to me from wherever he'd gone in his head.

"That was..."

"Mm-hm," I hummed, kissing the apple of his cheek and then the bridge of his nose.

"That..."

I snorted lightly before pulling back to look at him. "It was all right?"

He rolled his eyes, a quintessential Stevie maneuver that made me laugh. Had I ever laughed this much in a relationship before?

"No. It sucked. I demand a redo. Gimme a fucking break."

And another eye roll for good measure. His purple locks were whipped into a giant beehive tangle, and I wanted to work the knots out with my fingers. But I needed to do a little housekeeping first. I reached for the edge of the condom and pulled out of him carefully, disengaging from his embrace so I could dispose of the condom and fetch a wet cloth for him.

When I wandered back from the bathroom, I took a moment to appreciate the sight of him naked and sprawled out in limp pleasure in my bed.

"Why are you staring at me like a creeper?"

I climbed back onto the bed and stretched out next to him, reaching out to wash him off with the cloth. His smile turned to a shy grin while I worked until I flung the cloth away and pulled him close to me.

"I meant what I said. I love you. That wasn't just sex talk. I need you to know that."

Stevie's hand came out to caress my jaw. "Just out of curiosity, do you have a life insurance policy?"

I blinked at him.

"Kidding. I'm kidding. I'm feeling a little high right now, ignore me. Okay, maybe don't ignore me when I say this part. I love you too. But..."

My stomach dropped. "But?"

"No, I was calling you a butt. I love you too, Butt."

I blinked at him again. This was going to take some getting used to.

"Evan," he said softly. "I'm so fucking happy. I get stupid when I'm happy. Forgive me. Well, maybe instead of forgiving me, you could just... I don't know... get used to it? The weirdness, I mean. Because it doesn't really end. It's kind of... permanently attached to my personality."

I fingered the purple tangles. "I love your personality. But..."

"But?" Those little worry wrinkles appeared on his smooth forehead again.

"No, I was calling you a butt. I love your personality, Butt."

He smacked me in the shoulder. "I'm the funny one. You'd do well to remember that, Chief."

"I will. And I'll get used to your teasing. Your happiness is all I need, Stevie. If you're happy, I'm perfect."

We snuggled against each other, idly running fingers along skin and exploring each other until I heard his stomach grumble.

"We missed dinner. C'mon. Let's see what we can scrounge up."

After pulling on our jeans, we made our way into the kitchen where I found a frozen tub of baked ziti leftover from a batch I'd made at the fire house the week before. I placed it in the microwave and set the table, offering Stevie an assortment of drinks before inviting him to have a seat at the kitchen table.

As soon as he sat on the wooden chair, he hissed and hopped back up again.

"Whiskey tango foxtrot," he howled. "That bites. Motherfucker. Where did you get this piece-of-shit chair?"

Smothering a laugh, I said, "I made it. It's a basic chair, baby. I'm afraid the problem is with your delicate derriere and not the chair."

I wandered over to pull him into my arms, reaching down to rub his cute cheeks through the denim. "You want me to get you some softer pants? I might have a pair of bike shorts to pad this tush for you until you're feeling better."

"Stop laughing. This wasn't in the manual."

"What manual?" I asked with another chuckle. He was even more enticing when he pouted.

"The Bottom's Book of Banging," he said with a sniff before reaching up to toy with one of my nipples. "Don't tell me you've never read it. That's how I knew to look for a sugar daddy like you. The book says older men aren't strong enough to do too much damage to your—"

"What the fuck are you talking about?" I sputtered, cutting him off.

He lifted an eyebrow and smirked at me. "I thought you said you were going to get used to the weirdness?"

He was going to be the death of me.

"I did, Butt."

17

STEVIE

AFTER WE DEMOLISHED the pasta dish, Evan acted like the grown-up he was and brought up the topic I'd been avoiding all day.

"Who has Willow tonight?"

"Dina and her mom. The twins' birthday is today, so they're having a school-night sleepover. Dina will get them on the bus in the morning. I was kind of hoping to stay here with you. If that's okay, I mean."

Evan scooted his chair over and turned so my knees were between his open thighs. He reached for my hands and held them in his lap. "Of course it is, sweetheart. If I had my way, you'd stay here every night from now on. I want you to consider this your home whether I'm here or not. There's no pressure or anything, just know you're welcome here always. Now that you have a key, you don't even need to ask."

I scrabbled over to his lap and straddled him so I could show my appreciation in kisses. We finally made our way over to the sofa in the main room before settling down again with me all up in his grill. I wanted to be as close to him as I could get, even if the conversation wasn't going to be easy.

"I would love to stay here more often, but after last night... I can't trust my mom to be there for Willow. I don't know what her problem is lately, but…"

Evan's hands tightened on my back, pulling me closer against him. "You know the guy who runs the Vape Snake is a known heroin dealer, right?"

My stomach dropped. I'd heard rumors the guy was shady as hell, but hearing it confirmed by someone who worked close to law enforcement was a completely different thing. "Shit. Well, maybe that explains why she quit."

"What happened to her job at Valley Cross Cement? How'd she get hooked up at the vape shop?"

"She lost her job after Kade got arrested. When he finally had to start serving his time, she took his part-time position there," I explained.

"Does she usually leave Willow home alone?"

I could see the concern in his face. "Well, no, but…"

"I hope you're not calling me a butt—"

"No, no. I'm sorry. It's just… I mean, I want to say no. I want to say she never does. But that's the second time she's done it in the past two weeks." Evan's expression got stormier, so I hurried to reassure him. "I didn't know. Willow told me this morning when I interrogated her about it."

"Babe, I'm a mandatory reporter. That means I have to report child neglect within forty-eight hours. I obviously didn't want to do anything without talking to you first, but I can't just let it stand. She needs appropriate supervision."

My heart thundered in my chest. "I know. But, Evan… if you report us to CPS…"

He pressed a kiss to my forehead. "It wouldn't be you. It would be your mom. Stevie, I'm afraid she could have gotten into some bad shit if she was working with the people at that vape shop. Has she ever used?"

I shook my head. "No. Not that I've ever noticed. I swear, Evan. She doesn't even really drink that much. She's just depressed because of Kade going to jail."

He pulled me against his chest and tucked my head under his chin. "Do you want me to talk to her? Or would that make things worse? Hell, maybe we should see if we can get her in to see a doctor. Maybe she needs that kind of help."

Bless him for trying to give her the benefit of the doubt, but I knew the truth. My mom was making sketchy choices because she'd been completely gutted by Kade's conviction. She'd gone from a tough and hardworking mom to a woman who'd given up on everything. She simply didn't seem to give a shit anymore.

"I think maybe I should be the one to talk to her. But can you be there too? Just in case she doesn't take me seriously?"

"Of course. Do you want to go tonight while Willow is gone?"

I felt my nerves kick up. "I don't know if she's there. She never came home last night, and she's not returning my messages."

"Then we'll wait. As long as we know Willow is in good hands, it's not a rush."

He continued to stroke my hair and rub my back, dropping kisses onto my face here and there. After several minutes of comfortable silence, he brought up another dicey topic.

"What were you doing in Dallas?"

Fuck.

How the hell did I answer that without lying to him? If I told him I was dancing at a club, I'd seem like a negligent ass. If I told him I was *working* at a club, he'd ask what kind of work. And if I told him I was a go-go dancer... well, I didn't want to find out how he'd react. The man was clearly the jealous type.

"Working," I said calmly. I could do nonchalant. I could nonchalant the shit out of this.

"Doing what?"

"Oh, uh... I don't want to say."

He set me forward on his lap so he could see my face. His was stormy as hell. I raced to explain. Kind of.

"It wasn't anything illegal. I swear."

"Then why won't you tell me?"

"You're going to get mad, and I'm just not sure about this job yet. It's... I'm trying to become a bartender."

Truth. That was the truth.

"Why would that make me mad?"

He wasn't buying my bullshit, so I was going to have to do a much better job selling it. "I assume you're going to lecture me about being on the road home late at night." I lifted an eyebrow at him.

Gotcha.

"I am! It's dangerous. I can tell you a million stories about fatal accidents that happen in the middle of the night."

I lifted the other eyebrow. "What about me being an adult?"

"It's not you I'm worried about," he lied. "It's the other crazies on the road that late."

I didn't have any eyebrows left to raise, so I pulled out the big gun. "Okay, Daddy."

His face froze in horror at the name. "*No.*"

"But, Daddy..."

"*No.* Jesus fuck."

I stuck out my bottom lip in a pout. "What will you do if I misbehave, Daddy?"

"*I am not your father.*"

"Say it again, but this time call me Luke."

He finally snorted with laughter and grabbed me in a chokehold as if he was going to give me a noogie. I pulled out of his reach easily. "Touch the hair with disrespect and you lose petting privileges," I grumbled. "Believe me, you do *not* want to lose Stevie petting privileges."

"No, I do not."

We settled back down on the sofa, our lips finding each other again before long. Conversation came to an amicable end as our mouths and hands explored each other's bodies well into the night before Evan took mercy on me and let me fall asleep in his nice big bed surrounded by his warm embrace.

❧

THERE WAS a bad brush fire on Walnut Farm the following day that took the Hobie FD all day and into the night to contain. Everyone assumed it had started after some high school kids had neglected to properly extinguish a bonfire since it was the site of most of the town's bonfire nights. But whatever the cause, the result was no Chief Paige in the bakery or in my pants. Which sucked or didn't as it turned out.

That afternoon I stopped by the hospital and quit my job at the coffee cart. If things at Feathers were going to work out, I wouldn't be able to juggle another overnight job at the same time. And the tips alone at Feathers far outstripped the measly hourly wage at the coffee cart even when I considered the fuel cost of driving to and from Dallas.

But more important than any of it was Willow. I left the hospital and headed home to get there before the school bus did. There was no sign of my mother having come home the night before, so I tried her cell phone again. Still no luck. I tried desperately not to think of her doing something stupid. I packed Willow up and drove to the vape shop just to see if anyone there knew where she might be, but I didn't have any luck. The stoner behind the counter didn't even act like he knew who she was, so I gave up and went home.

By Friday morning, I was dreading Evan's call. I knew he'd ask about my mother, and I'd have to tell him she was MIA. He'd already stretched the rules by not calling CPS after finding Willow home alone, and I would never ask him to cover for us twice in the same week. As it was, I already felt awful for putting him in this situation.

To add to my stress, I was scheduled to work again that night at Feathers. Darius planned on putting me behind the bar but said he couldn't guarantee it. Either way, I needed the tips. I'd already signed Willow up for dance before finding out about my mom losing her job. As great as it was to see Willow so excited about the lessons, I knew I now needed to keep working hard to make enough money to pay each month's dance tuition on top of all the other obligations we had. There was no telling whether Mom would be helping with the next month's rent, so I had to assume it was all on me.

The stress of managing everything and keeping secrets from Evan had me in knots all day until he finally called me midafternoon after I'd come in from getting Willow off the bus.

"Hey," I said, wandering back to the privacy of my room. My stomach jangled with nerves, but the sound of his familiar voice soothed me anyway.

"Hey, sweetheart. Did you make it home okay from work? I stopped by Sugar Britches, but Nico said you'd already left."

"Yeah, I had to get home before the bus came. Is everything okay at the fire house?"

"Mm-hm. Catching up on all the work we missed yesterday with the Walnut Farm fire. Things are slammed over here. Listen… I have this thing tonight. I'm supposed to meet up with some buddies of mine in the city to celebrate an engagement. I was thinking I might cancel since I haven't seen you…"

"No. I have to work tonight anyway, and Willow is staying with the twins again. You go ahead and have fun with your friends."

There was silence for several beats. I knew he was dying to ask where I was working, but he probably realized it would be crossing a boundary I'd set the other night.

"Do you want to ride with me to the city?" he asked instead.

I thought of him dropping me off in front of the gay club. The mental image in my head included sirens and explosives… maybe an arrest warrant or two.

"No, thanks. I'll be fine."

"Stevie…" He sighed. "Are you sure I can't help you with some money? You can consider it a loan if you want to. I just—"

"We haven't been going out long enough for that, Evan," I said. "And you know it."

"No, I don't know it. I want to help ease your burdens. Please let me help you, sweetheart."

His voice was low and tempting, but I stayed strong. "Maybe later. After we've been together a while. Right now I just can't, okay?"

Evan paused. "All right. I won't push. Will you come home to my house after you're done?"

I was too busy smiling to myself to answer right away.

"Or at least text me to tell me you made it home safely," he said more softly. "Please."

"I'll come to your place. I'd like that," I admitted. "I miss you, Chief."

"I miss you too, beautiful."

I bounced through the rest of my afternoon and evening with an extra spring in my step. Despite the continued absence of my mother, I felt like maybe things were going to be okay. At least I wasn't alone anymore. I had Evan Paige on my side, and he wanted to be a part of my life. It was the first time besides becoming friends with Sassy Wilde that I'd truly no longer felt alone.

Tonight I was finally going to get to work behind the bar, which meant I'd be able to tell Evan I was working as a barback in hopes of being a bartender soon, and it wouldn't be a lie.

As soon as I could get ahead of the game financially, I'd have to look for a job that paid better than my hourly rate at Sugar Britches. As much as working at the bakery was my biggest selfish indulgence, I had to finally admit it didn't pay enough to help make up for my mom's job changes. I couldn't imagine telling Nico I could no longer work for him. The very idea of leaving all the people and the place that felt like home to me made me nauseous. But I wouldn't think about it yet. One thing at a time.

After dropping Willow off with Dina, I returned home and pulled on a sexy pair of skinny jeans and a tight, hot-pink tank that said *Power Bottoms For Jesus* on it. I had to admit to feeling a bit extra smug wearing it now that I was a legitimate bottom. A bottom in practice, not just imagination.

Hell, I was like the *king* of bottoms now. I'd had sex—bottoming, obvs—a sum total of one time. But that one time had been epic. And I'd bossed him around, hadn't I? I'd told him things like *more* and... ah... *more* again. And I'd commanded him to jimmy my prostate too. So, yeah. *Hell* yeah. I was a power bottom. I *owned* the title of power bottom.

I sauntered out of my apartment and straight into a pack of dudes with low-hanging jeans and white tank tops looking shifty next to a tricked-out Honda Civic hatchback with undercarriage lighting.

"'Sup," I said with a nod as I headed toward my Ford sedan, praying like hell those gangsters weren't going to peg me as gay. When I got into the car, I looked down at my lavender skinny jeans with artful slashes up and down the thighs and my super-gay tank and laughed my fucking ass off.

Sure, Stevie. You totally pass as straight. Straight out of a pride parade.

Sometimes I wondered if maybe growing up, I'd taken the whole "Be Yourself" thing a little too far. My mom had gone through a phase of playing Sara Bareilles's song "Brave" on repeat for like ten weeks straight a few years ago. And before that, I'd been given a beat-up copy of a colorful book by a daycare teacher that told a story of a colorful patchwork elephant who didn't match all the gray ones. It was the only book that had ever been mine and not borrowed from the library or shared with my brother. I'd read it a million times. Maybe I'd read it so much, I'd turned into Elmer the Patchwork Elephant and the dudes in the apartment parking lot were the regular gray ones.

How sad for them.

Katy Perry's "Firework" was playing on the radio when I turned on the car. I rolled my windows down despite the February air, cranked up the volume just as she sang, "You're original, cannot be replaced," and sang my fool head off as I drove out of the lot.

I was in such a fantastic mood when I arrived at Feathers, even discovering I had to dance that night didn't bring me down.

Until I saw Chief Fucking Paige sitting in the front row and panicked.

18

EVAN

I was in a pissy mood when I met up with the guys. Everyone gave me hell for being in a funk, so I tried to fake it despite doing a terrible job of it.

"Seriously, Paige," one of my old coworkers said with a frown. "What the hell's wrong with you tonight? I thought you were cool with going to a club."

I looked up at the entrance to the dance club they'd chosen. It was fine. I was happy to help Cody celebrate and catch up with all the guys, but I was having a hard time not worrying about Stevie. He was killing himself to make enough money to support his family when I was sitting on a fat savings account I'd accumulated after twenty-five years of earning more money than I spent on just myself. My house had been paid for by an inheritance from my grandfather, and some of my woodworking projects brought in money here and there. My tastes weren't extravagant, and I lived in a small town with few temptations for big expenditures. So why wouldn't he let me help him? And why did I feel like offering him money again would make him feel like some kind of rent boy?

"Dude, focus. You almost ran into that guy."

My head came up to see the big bearded man scoff at me over his shoulder as I made my way through the crowd toward a table someone had saved for us. The place was packed, and music thumped hard enough to make me worry for my heart.

Someone pushed a drink into my hand and pointed to the dance number about to start on the main stage.

Within seconds one of the dancers on stage caught my attention. A small, slender guy with pale skin and natural rhythm. Each of the featured dancers who emerged from behind a curtain had an elaborate feathered mask, jewels and feathers seemingly glued to their upper chest, and a large plume of feathers attached to the back of a skimpy pair of boy shorts. It was a riot of color, all of the dancers displaying their individual shade. But one of the dancers was in all black. He was the littlest guy up there, and instead of jewels on his chest, he wore black feathered epaulettes. His mask, shorts, and tail feathers were all the same silky black, strikingly set off by his pale winter skin.

He was stunning.

Even though he was small, his body was curved with defined dancer's muscles, and I couldn't take my eyes off it. He was transported by the music—almost like he wasn't actually there with us but on another plane. He was in his own world, caressed by the rhythm and one with the beat. He displayed an intoxicating blend of grace and strength. Every sultry roll of his hips showed off slender abs. Every deep, open-legged squat showed the power of his quads and calves. When he spun around, I saw sinewy back muscles over a slim waist, a waist that would feel so fucking amazing between my hands. A waist that *did* feel amazing between my hands.

"Holy fuck," I breathed.

"You okay, Chief?" someone at my table asked.

"That's my boyfriend," I said without thinking. The table of guys hooted and hollered, several of them claiming he was their boyfriend too, assuming I'd been joking.

"No, you assholes. That's actually my boyfriend."

Before I decide what to do, my phone buzzed for the third time in as many minutes in my pocket. I wasn't on call, but as the chief of the Hobie FD, it was part of my job to always be reachable.

The text on the screen was from Sassy.

West found Stevie's mom on a 72-hour psych hold at hospital. Stevie not answering phone. What do I do? Worried about Willow!

I glanced up at the beautiful man dancing his heart out on stage.

Willow at Dina's. I know where Stevie is. I'll get him and bring him to hospital.

Leaning over toward Cody, I apologized for leaving. "Sorry, but something's come up. I'll take you and Eric for dinner soon. Would love to introduce you to Stevie," I said, nodding toward the black-feathered dancer. Cody's eyes widened in appreciation of my boyfriend's stunning form shimmying to the beat of the club track, and I had to restrain myself from growling at him to put his damned eyeballs back in their sockets.

As I walked toward the bar to inquire about how to meet up with Stevie after his dance routine, I saw all the patrons in the place salivating over my man. Did it make me jealous? Hell yes. Did I also feel incredibly smug that he was mine and mine alone? Fuck yes.

But now wasn't the time to strut around like an asshole. I had to find him and tell him the news before taking him to the hospital and most likely staying with him while he had to deal with some tough realities.

"What do you want to drink?" the bartender asked.

"Oh, no. I need to meet one of your dancers after he's done," I shouted over the music, thumbing over my shoulder at the stage. The bartender and at least three men around me snorted.

"Don't we all. Save your breath. Unless you've got large bills, you ain't getting any from those young guys," one of the men said.

I ground my teeth together before trying again. "The dancer in the black feathers is my boyfriend. There's been a family emergency. His mom is in the hospital."

The bartender's smirk faded, and he nodded. "Let me get Darius. He'll help."

I was waiting in the manager's office when he brought Stevie in.

He wore a pink tank over his black boy shorts and looked like a puppy who was getting ready to be bopped on the nose with a newspaper.

"C'mere," I said gruffly, reaching for him and pulling him into a tight hug. "I love you. You were fucking amazing up there. Stunning. I can't even tell you how proud I am of you."

"Really?" he asked in a breathy voice. "You're not mad at me?"

I put him at arm's length and held on to his shoulders so I could look into his eyes. "I wish you'd felt comfortable enough to tell me what you were doing, but no. I'm not mad at you. I'm upset, but only because you're trying so hard to support your family that it's going to break you down one of these days. I want to help you, baby. Financially, I mean. I don't want you killing yourself working three jobs. If you want to dance here because you love it, then I'll support you one hundred percent. If you're doing it to make more money, though, we're going to talk, because you're burning out, sweetheart. But right now, we need to go."

"What do you mean? I can't go. I still have several hours left."

I cupped his face in my hands. "Your mom is in the hospital. Sassy tried to get a hold of you and texted me when she couldn't get you."

"Is that how you found me?"

"No, baby. I was here with the guys for Cody's bachelor party thing. I just so happened to see you up there right before she texted me."

"Wait, what? Mom's in the hospital?" My words about the situation seemed to finally sink in. "What the hell happened? Is she okay? Where has she been?"

I ran my hands up and down his arms. "It's a psychiatric hold. I don't know the details. That's why we need to go. Grab your things and I'll drive us in your car. I rode to town with one of the guys."

Stevie made his way back to the dancer lounge in a daze, emerging a minute later with a backpack. He still only wore the tank and boy shorts, so I quickly slipped my jacket off and wrapped it around his shoulders while taking the backpack from him.

We didn't talk on the drive back. Stevie tried calling the hospital to get more information, but they were tight-lipped since he couldn't prove he was related to her until he showed his ID. When we were only fifteen minutes out from the hospital, we finally got a hold of the doctor in charge of her case.

"Someone found her standing on the edge of an overpass," he said in a sympathetic voice over speakerphone after asking Stevie if he knew of her drug use history and hearing his emphatic *no*. "She wasn't responsive to law enforcement's attempts to talk to her, so they involved emergency medical help. We determined enough risk to her safety to put her on a seventy-two-hour hold. Jodi asked us not to contact her family members, but it's my understanding she's now spoken to Dr. Wilde and rescinded that request."

"Is she going to be okay?" Stevie asked. I reached over and clasped his hand, squeezing it tightly.

"I think so. We've gone through some counseling already and done quite a bit of intake information gathering. Of course we'd love to talk to you as well, Mr. Devore, but as of right now I'd say she's suffering from severe depression that can most likely be treated successfully with a combination of counseling and medication."

Stevie glanced at me before looking out the window again. "I don't... I mean we don't..." he exhaled. "She doesn't have insurance."

"I'll cover it," I said firmly before he could argue. "It's important, and I have the money."

"There are some programs that can help also," the doctor continued. "I'm happy to put you in touch with a community liaison who can steer you in the right direction. In the meantime, why don't we plan on meeting for a joint counseling session tomorrow at four if that works for you?"

"Yes, sir," Stevie said, nodding. "We'll be there. Thank you so much for your help. If you see her before then, please tell her I love her and have everything under control at home."

"I certainly will."

We continued the drive to my house without speaking. Stevie held on to my hand with both of his like it was a lifeline. When I pulled into the driveway and turned off the ignition, Stevie turned to me.

"Evan, I need your help. I don't think I can do this by myself anymore."

Hearing him say those words was almost more meaningful than hearing him tell me he loved me. Because I knew he finally trusted me enough to let go. He finally accepted that I was on his side and he didn't need to be alone anymore.

"Sweetheart, you don't need to do anything by yourself ever again."

19

STEVIE

WE SPENT hours that night making plans. Evan treated me like an equal the entire time, asking me how I wanted to handle Willow's custodial situation while my mom got treatment. I told him about all of my jobs and exactly how much money I made, including a brief rundown of our expenses including the new dance lessons commitment which, in hindsight, was a bad decision.

"I disagree," Evan said in a brusque voice. "Willow deserves something special that's just for her. And we can afford it. The dance lessons stay."

He was making a list on a legal pad where we sat at the kitchen table, and he emphasized his point by underlining the Valley Cross Dance Studio entry twice. I noticed my jaw begin to tremble.

"Don't be nice," I warned him. "I can't handle it right now, Butt."

He reached over and ran long fingers through my hair. "Too bad. I'm going to *nice* the hell out of you. If you need to cry, then cry. I can take it."

The tears came quickly. Of course they did. Because the stupid fucker hadn't heeded my warning. "It's all your fault," I wailed. "I told you not to be that guy. The nice one. The *stupid* fucking nice one."

His mouth dropped open in surprise, and he rushed to wipe my tears away with his thumbs. "Shit. Stevie, fuck. I didn't realize you were really going to cry like this. Make it stop. Baby, please."

His face was creased with concern as he continued to apologize. It was funny, really. Clearly he wasn't used to crying boyfriends. I hiccupped and hitched several breaths before wailing again. It was a doozie, and even my sugar daddy frantically scooping me a bowl of mint chocolate chip didn't make a dent in the waterworks.

Evan finally stopped in the middle of the kitchen with his hands up in surrender and a panic-stricken expression on his face. "Please stop crying, I beg you." His voice was hoarse, and I thought maybe his own eyes were wet. "You're breaking my heart. I can't take it." He knelt on the floor and laid his head in my lap. "Please."

He really was amazing, and he clearly loved the hell out of me.

"You think you can handle a hot mess," I teased, reaching for another napkin to blow my nose with. "But you're a lightweight when the rubber meets the road, Chief."

He looked up at me in a sudden lightbulb moment. "The workshop!"

"I'm not tackling the green dragon right now. Not saying I'd be opposed to some healthy distraction, but I was thinking of another kind of woodworking, to be honest."

"No! My workshop has heating and air-conditioning as well as a full bathroom and a finished attic space with the dormer windows. It's big enough to convert it into a two-bedroom apartment really easily."

What the heck was he talking about? Rental property? What did that have to do with—

"Your mom and Willow could live there so we could help out with Willow and keep an eye on your mom. It would mean no more paying rent, so she could have time to work on getting better instead of stressing about getting another job."

My head spun with the idea. "Evan, we can't possibly—"

His hand covered my mouth. "Please don't say no yet. Let's talk it through like we agreed to do about all this stuff. We're partners now, remember?"

I thought about what it would be like living in a converted garage apartment on Evan's property. "You wouldn't have any privacy. If my family and I lived in your workshop apartment, you'd never have time alone."

Evan stared at me like I was an alien. "No, sweetheart. You'd be living with me here in our house. The apartment would be for your mom and Willow."

Was he asking me to move in with him? More than that, was he basically asking my entire family to move in with him?

"Are you insane?" I croaked. "Why would you do that? You have everything right now. A great job, good money, property, solitude, a little twink on the side..."

His eyes narrowed. "You'd better be joking about the side bit. And all the rest is bullshit if you're not here with me. Willow and I get along great. I haven't officially met your mom before, but I'd love a chance to help her because I love you and presumably you love her. There will be conditions of her staying here though. She'll have to show you respect and pursue treatment of some kind if that's what the doctor recommends. If she can't do those two things..."

"She can. Well, at least the respecting me part. She's kind of changed her tune toward me since Kade went away. I think she's finally realizing that I can be weird, gay, *and* reliable at the same time."

We talked through what would need to be done to the workshop before we could move them into it.

"What about your woodworking?" I asked. I couldn't imagine asking him to give up his hobby for my family.

"I have a three-car garage and one truck. Even with your car here, we can park in the driveway and move my woodshop into the garage until we think of another solution. Who knows? Maybe I can build a new workshop on the other side of the house where that old boathouse used to be."

When the subject of my jobs came back around, I sat up straight. "I've been thinking about this a lot. I think I want to ask Nico to give me Rox's old job as manager of the bakery."

"I thought Nico was the bakery manager."

I nodded. "He is, but I think it was out of some kind of leftover guilt toward his sister. Now that his tattoo shop is growing so quickly, he's stretched pretty thin. I've always thought I couldn't handle the responsibility, but I can. And I deserve it. I want that job, Evan. Sugar Britches is a part of me, and I know every customer who comes through there. There's no person better to manage the place than me. I may not have a college degree yet, but I know lots of smart people who can help me learn what I need to know in the meantime."

The hearts in Evan's eyes were comical.

"You're a badass," he said. "I'm so fucking proud of you. If he knows what's good for him, Nico won't even let you get the proposition out of your mouth before he says hell yes. And you know I'll do anything to help. Even though my degree is in Fire and Emergency Services Administration, it's still considered a degree from A&M's College of Business in San Antonio."

I lifted an eyebrow. "You trying to impress me, Chief?"

"You trying to flirt with me, gorgeous?"

I climbed onto his lap to straddle him, sliding my hands over his wide, muscular shoulders and appreciating the salt-and-pepper stubble on his cheeks by nuzzling my face against it.

"Always."

We left the legal pad on the table and made our way to the bedroom where one or the other of us worked all the wood to our mutual satisfaction.

EVAN'S EPILOGUE

"Satan's ballsac, it's as hot as a naked firefighter out here," Stevie mumbled under his breath as he ripped open the top of the first bakery box from the stack we'd just unloaded off the hand truck.

"Baby, there are kids and families here. Language," I reminded him.

He glared at me. The purple hair I loved so much was swirled into a Shoney Boy swoop and shellacked to within an inch of its life. Navy blue liquid eyeliner on the edges of his violet eyes meant I couldn't keep myself from staring at them even though I got to live with those amazing eyes every day. Pink lip gloss had been chewed off his bottom lip by me when I'd gotten him alone in the bakery kitchen twenty minutes earlier. The man was a goddamned tasty treat.

"You're so fucking hot." I sighed.

"Right? That's what I'm saying. It's like Channing Tatum in *Magic Mike* out here. I shouldn't have gone commando. Everything is sticking to... places."

He continued to set pastries out on trays under the white tent canopy Sugar Britches had set up for the Hobie Hootenanny. Nico's tattoo tent was right next to it, and he'd already stopped what he was doing at least three times to come over and take Stevie by the shoulders to thank him. This time was no different.

"Please don't ever leave me," Nico had said across the white-clothed table that formed a makeshift barrier between the two spaces. "I mean, I'm already paying you as much as I can, so don't use this to negotiate more, but promoting you to manager was the best management decision you ever made for me."

I laughed and winked at Stevie when his mouth dropped open in surprise. By the third time Nico told him he loved him, Stevie started his usual snarky back talk.

"I'm not having sex with you no matter how much you flatter me. Clearly you're a bottom, and that simply wouldn't work," Stevie had said with a sniff.

Nico and West stared at him. "That's patently false," West asserted.

"TMI, Dr. Wilde," I said with a shudder. "No one out here wants those details."

Nico grabbed his husband's shoulder and pushed him closer to Stevie. "Tell him about this morning. Tell him how hard I—"

West clapped a hand over his husband's indignant pout. "La-la-la enough of that nonsense. Suffice it to say, Nico's an animal in the sack, and we change things up at the Wilde house. There, you satisfied?"

Nico narrowed his eyes at Stevie for good measure before pulling West's hand away and kissing it quickly before dropping it.

Stevie glanced up from where he'd begun setting out more cupcakes. "Huh? What are you going on about? Can't you see I'm busy over here? Go ink some people. Or whatever. I've got cakes to sell."

He wore the new turquoise bakery T-shirt with the Sugar Britches logo emblazoned across the front in hot pink. It looked amazing on him even though he'd taken the liberty of cutting off the sleeves and tying the excess bulk of the shirt into a tight knot at his lower back to show off his narrow flat stomach and adorable, tight ass in snug lavender shorts. I'd pretty much had a hard-on since breakfast.

Stevie caught me staring. "Go put out a fire or something. You're giving me the creeps."

"I'd like to be giving you something else."

His eyes flicked up to the heavens. "Blessed Virgin, grant me peace or I swear to fucking god…"

"I love you."

"Tell me something I don't know," he said, going back to his work. He took great pride in making sure everything was just so. He'd been planning this festival display for weeks, and I was thrilled to finally watch him see it all come to fruition. Especially after the challenging few months we'd had.

This month things finally seemed to be on an even keel. Jodi had been doing very well with a combination of antidepressants and twice-a-week counseling sessions. She'd been downright relieved when we'd suggested moving her and Willow to Hobie from Valley Cross and was finally well enough to start a new job working for Leonard Fickle at the accounting office here in Hobie. Leonard had been in dire straits after his wife left him since she'd also been his office manager. From the rumors flying around town, Leonard had taken one look at Jodi Devore during the interview and forgotten Carrie-Ann Clapper-Fickle had ever existed.

The three of us had made a point of driving Willow back to Valley Cross every day for school until the school year ended so she could finish out first grade with her friends. Even though she'd be switching to Hobie Elementary the following month, we still promised to keep her in dance lessons with the twins over in Valley Cross. We also reminded them that while it seemed far away, they'd all be reunited again in middle and high school since Valley Cross and Hobie had plans to merge their schools when the big new ones were built the following year.

More than anything, Willow was Willow. She radiated happiness and joy the way Stevie did. Having her around all the time made all our lives better and more fun. We'd quickly discovered her desire to have regular family dinners together most nights and had made it a priority as much as possible. Those dinners had turned out to be the making of our little family.

Things between Jodi and me had started out rough. She'd originally tried to be the parent in our little unique family until we'd discovered I was older than she was. That had helped calm her down and allowed her to let go of being in charge of everything all the time. Ever since she'd relaxed her attitude, she'd seemed to flourish. I wondered if she realized how much happier she seemed now that she didn't have to carry the load herself. Now that Stevie was working more hours at the bakery, sometimes Jodi and I would find ourselves hanging out together in the afternoons with a glass of wine out on the dock while Willow splashed around in the lake. I'd begun starting shifts earlier at the fire house so I could be home in plenty of time to help ferry Willow around wherever she needed to go, whether it was summer day camp, dance, or to visit the twins for a sleepover.

I realized I'd flaked out and missed what Stevie had asked me. "I'm sorry, what?" I asked.

He smirked at me. "Losing your hearing, big daddy? Already? I said tell me something I don't know."

I chuckled. He'd handed me the perfect opening just as Willow and Jodi appeared under the tent. I took a step back to get some space.

"I have a ring in my pocket," I said. "That's something you don't know."

Willow giggled and slapped her hand over her mouth. Both the ladies knew what I was planning since I'd asked both their permissions the night before while Stevie was working late at the shop.

Stevie looked up with his familiar forehead crinkles of confusion. "What? A ring? What kind of..."

His face dropped into utter shock and his eyes widened comically. "OH NO YOU DIDN'T."

"Oh yes I did."

I knelt down on one knee, praying nothing popped or cracked on the way down while I was already feeling vulnerable. "Steven January Devore."

His eyes narrowed and hissed, "You shut your whore mouth."

He hated his middle name even though I thought it was delightfully simple. His mother rolled her eyes and mouthed *I'm so sorry* at him.

"My life before you was like the gray elephant," I began. "And then I met you. Now my life is an explosion of color. I get to live this life with you in full color all day every day, and it's been the greatest gift I've ever received." My voice broke as I saw my mom and dad making their way through the crowd toward us. They'd met Stevie, Jodi, and Willow already, but I'd invited them for the Hootenanny because I wanted them to see Stevie shine.

"Baby, I love you more than I can possibly express in words. You are capable and smart, fun and loving. You make me... us... laugh every single day, and I know you are going to do amazing things with your life. I want to be along for the ride if you'll let me. Stevie, sweetheart, will you marry me?"

Navy blue liquid eyeliner streaked down his face, and his hair flopped over as he shook his head in wonder.

"Yes, but..."

My mother and a few other onlookers gasped. Sassy stood behind Nico and giggled because she obviously knew the joke.

"Don't call me a butt when I'm proposing marriage to you," I said softly with a smile, still looking up at him from where I knelt on the hard ground.

His hands were in front of his mouth, and his forehead was creased again with the strength of his tears. "I told you I was a hot mess."

"I'm a firefighter, sweetheart. Hot messes are my life's blood. I eat hot messes for breakfast. I have a degree in how to handle hot messes."

"I love you so much, Evan," he whispered through his snotty tears. "Of course I'll marry you, Chief."

The crowd that had quickly gathered around us cheered as I

lurched up and grabbed my love around the waist, kissing and hugging him as I lifted him off his feet and spun him around.

After I set him down, I pulled out the ring to slide onto his finger. It was charcoal tungsten with a tiny purple pinstripe running through it. He let out an "eep" when he saw it and clapped his hands with excitement. "You got this for me? I love purple!"

I looked at his hair, his eyes, his shorts. "I know, baby. That's why I picked this one. I hoped you'd love it since you'll have to wear it forever."

He jumped at me again, throwing his arms around my neck and his legs around my waist. I held on to him as if my life depended on it.

Because it did.

STEVIE'S EPILOGUE

Later That Night

I couldn't take my eyes off the sweetest engagement ring on the planet. "Tell me again where you found it," I asked, sliding my foot up his torso in the cool, bubbly bathwater. We sat on opposite ends of our enormous bath pool as I called the jetted tub in our master bath. We'd both been covered in sweat, sugar, and festival grime when we'd finally staggered home half an hour earlier from the Hootenanny. As much as I'd wanted to hump my future husband, I needed to wash the crowd off me first.

As I'd run the bath, Evan had run back downstairs to mix us up some icy-cold cocktails before the two of us lowered ourselves into the refreshing bath.

"Guy selling corn on the side of the road makes 'em," he said, soaping up my foot with the bar of sporty man-smell soap he used. I normally used a floral-scented body wash, but whenever we bathed together, the dude marked me with his man-scent like I was some kind of conquest.

Of course, I secretly loved it.

I flicked water at him with my fingertips. "Liar. You had Tibetan monks pray it into existence."

His deep laugh filled the bathroom and my cock.

"Close. I got it at the pawn shop. You know, the one next to the Sip and Save?"

"Never mind. You're impossible. And, quite frankly, you're skating the line into dad-joke territory."

"Mpfh," he grumbled, causing me to bark out a laugh.

"Grunting like an old man doesn't help your case, gramps."

He pulled my foot up and took a bite of my big toe.

"Aiyeee! If you're going to put body parts in your mouth, I have better suggestions."

You might be surprised how quickly an aging silver fox can move when he's properly motivated. I was washed, dried, and shoved face-first against the bathroom wall in 2.5 seconds.

"What just happened?" I squeaked.

"You dangled a carrot in front of me," he growled in my ear. Oh my sexy hell.

"And are you hungry?" I drawled, shaking my ass against his very large, very hard carrot.

"Starving. Gonna eat you out as a matter of fact."

My head spun. Evan putting his mouth on my hole was my favorite. Hell, who was I kidding? Evan putting his mouth anywhere on me was my favorite. But tonight was his night to be worshipped.

"Big daddy?"

"Stop it. You're making my boner deflate."

"Don't worry. I got West to give me some of those little blue—"

"Say the word pills and I'm pulling out the ball gag."

I turned around in his embrace and wrapped my arms around his neck. "But then you'd miss out on what my mouth wants to do to your carrot." I tried for sultry, but I wasn't sure I was able to pull it off.

"What are you even talking about right now? I thought I was going to eat your ass and then fuck you up against the wall. That was a good plan. I like that plan. Why are we talking about vegetables?"

Now it was my turn to drop to my knees. "Because I'm very good at eating my vegetables." I took his big fat cock into my mouth, running my hand up his silver-and-black happy trail, across the bumps of his abdomen that were softened beautifully with age, and up to his nipples, which I knew from experience were pebbled and waiting for a light pinch.

I obliged.

"Jesus fuck," he hissed as I tongued the head and sucked his shaft into my wet mouth. His fingers came into my hair first thing, and sometimes I actually wondered if that was his favorite part of receiving oral sex from me. "More. Just like that. Love your sweet mouth."

His rumbly words of praise surrounded me with a heady combination of familiarity and hot-as-fuck excitement. When Evan Paige stood over me while I serviced him, it made my dick leak faster than ever. Despite his dominant position, it was never more apparent than when I was sucking his cock that I owned him completely. For some reason, kneeling at his feet and sucking him off made me high as a damned kite. He ceased being intimidating, controlled Chief Paige and became my lover Evan, the man who caressed my face and wiped my tears away when I took him too deep and gagged. The man who carried me gently into the bedroom when I was finished and spent on the floor. The sweet soul who curled his body around me the whole night through as if I was the most important jewel in his crown.

I fondled his balls and sucked on him until he was thrusting to the back of my throat and tightening his hold on my hair. Just before the point of no return, I pulled off and stood back up, reaching into a nearby drawer for a tube of lube and squirting out a good portion on my fingers while Evan gasped and sputtered his discontent at my abrupt departure.

"What... why... *baby*! I need you," he said through gasping breaths. His hand held his cock, squeezing at the base to hold off his climax.

"Want you to fuck me. Want you to finish inside me," I said as I finished a quickie prep session and threw myself face-first against the door the way he'd had me right after the bath. "Please." I wiggled my ass in invitation.

"Sweetest goddamned ass," he muttered, pulling my cheeks apart. "Good idea. He always has good ideas."

I wondered if he knew he was talking out loud. Before I could ask, he speared inside of me.

"Evan!" I cried as he nailed my prostate on the first stroke. "*Evan.*" This time it was a whimper as he reached around to stroke my cock as his teeth caught my earlobe in my favorite kind of love bite.

"Mine forever," he murmured into my ear like honey. "Love of my life."

I banged a fist against the wall and shoved my ass back to take in more of him. He grunted and slammed into me, saying something about me taking it. Yes, I would take anything he wanted to give. For ever and ever.

Strong feelings threatened to send me to my knees, but I was too exhausted from the big day to let it happen. So I poked the bear instead.

"Oh, honey," I groaned. "Is that all you got? You want to lie down and let me do the work? Been a long day. You're probably t—"

One hand clamped over my mouth while the other arm locked around my front like a vise, and he pounded into me, nailing my gland over and over and over until my release shot out of me against the bathroom wall and I nearly lost my tenuous hold on reality. My legs buckled and Evan followed me to the ground, continuing to fuck into me until his last strong thrust was accompanied by a roar of pleasure.

We lay there in a hot sticky mess on the floor, panting and heaving and, in my case, half-unconscious.

After a while spent dropping tiny kisses along my shoulder and down my spine, Evan finally moved us into the shower for a quick cleanup. I didn't pay much attention, just leaned against him to keep from falling down again.

He dried me off again and poured me into bed, turning off the light and climbing in behind me to spoon. I turned to face him, meeting his eyes in the dim moonlight coming through the edges of the blinds.

"Thank you for loving me," I said, slurring my words in exhaustion. "Every day I feel like I won the lottery. I can't wait until I'm your husband. I love you so much."

"I love you too, sweetheart. Get some sleep. We have another full day of the festival tomorrow, including Willow's dance routine."

"Wish I was dancing too," I murmured against his hairy chest. "I like dancing for you."

His hand brushed through my hair with such sweet affection, I felt myself drifting off even more with the comfort of his touch.

"Good," he said with a smile in his voice. "Then you won't mind I stopped by Feathers and convinced Darius to give me your old costume. I'm expecting a private show once things with the festival die down."

I thought back to the only night I'd gotten to wear the sexy ensemble. I'd fantasized a million times about getting a do-over for that night and having the chance to dance just for him.

"Mm-hm. Just for you though. I only shake my tail feathers for one person these days. I'm a one-bird feather-shaker. Ask anyone," I mumbled.

I didn't remember much after that except for the deep familiar rumbles of my favorite laugh as I slipped off to a dreamless sleep.

ARTHUR AND MAX

1

———————

ARTHUR

WHILE IT WASN'T my place to complain, a man such as myself had certain... needs. And I was sick and damned tired of watching Lior and his Felix all perfect and sex-drunk half the time when I, myself, was getting the sum total of zero love.

And by love, I meant sex.

And by sex, I meant hard fucking.

Because, as I said, a man had needs.

Standing at the Wilde wedding watching those two sweet old souls renew their lifelong commitment to each other was like something out of a dream. It was too good to be true, seeing them celebrate over forty years together as committed, loving life partners.

I spent the ceremony on the verge of inappropriate emotional leakage, but I successfully distracted myself with thoughts of the incredible wine Felix would sneak me at the reception later. He'd still not gotten used to having a manservant and treated me more like a bro than a valet. While most of the time I spurred his public attempts to be my bud, when it came to wine, I wasn't proud. I'd accept whatever the hell he saw fit to give me. The day Lio had explained we were going to Napa for a wedding, it was the Napa part I'd latched onto with a thudding heart.

Screw the wedding nonsense. I wanted to get taste the good stuff.

By the time the Marians and Wildes were three sheets—okay make that five or more sheets—to the wind, I was also sporting a silent but seductive buzz. And I was... *needful.*

There should be a better word for it besides horny. That word was so inelegant.

But dear god, if I was going to be forced into a room with dozens of beautiful gay men, what else did I expect to happen? It was like taking James Bond to Monaco and not letting him gamble. Unfair and unnatural.

From the very beginning, I'd had my eye on a cutie with dimples who turned out to be one of Felix's cousins. I would never in a million years *act* on my attraction to the man, of course, but I was definitely enjoying the view so long as he was around.

He was fairly short with slender muscles, and I only really knew about the muscles because I'd seen him in jogging tights and a fitted running top outside on a walking trail. Little white ear buds had stuck out bright against his inky black curls and half of his shirt had been rucked up, revealing one half of a luscious bottom that made my palms... also *needful.*

Later, the group of Marians and Wildes had all gathered in the lodge lobby for an impromptu cocktail hour and I'd overheard someone call him Max. I'd been tempted to ask Felix about him, but in the end, I'd tamped down the urge. Poor Felix was so distracted and anxious about performing his grandfathers' ceremony, I didn't want to give him something else to stress over.

And the "help" drooling over his adorable cousin was silliness Felix didn't need when two of the most important men in his life were getting ready to renew their vows.

So I asked Sassy Wilde. And got an ear full.

Apparently, sweet Max Wilde was unlucky in love like myself. In addition to being the victim of horrible bullying as a teen, he'd also had his heart smashed by his college boyfriend. Since then, at least according to his cousin Sassy, he'd scoffed at any attempt to set him up.

Which meant there was a slight possibility I could have no-strings sex with the adorable man without him wanting to dive into something more.

Because I was over forty and getting a little too old and set in my ways to consider anything serious. What kind of man would want to move into the royal palace with me anyway? No. I simply needed to scratch my itch.

And if I had one more glass of wine, maybe I'd be stupid enough to do it with a Wilde.

2

MAX

When I first saw Arthur, I thought he was a movie star. Maybe a friend of Aunt Jackie's or a famous friend of the Marians. He was beautiful in a mature way with salt and pepper hair and laugh lines to the side of his eyes. Then I'd realized who he was. Felix had told me all about Arthur.

He was the king's valet which was essentially the man who handled Felix's husband's personal affairs. Which meant the man lived in Europe—in a castle no less. Way, way out of my league.

But he was hot as hell.

And I was feeling so fucking sorry for myself at yet another Wilde wedding where I had absolutely zero chance of ever being the groom.

"Needs mores drinks," I muttered to no one in particular.

"The plural stage of Max's drunkenness has begun," Hallie shouted in triumph. "I loves plurals Maxes."

"I don'ts..." Whats weres we talkings abouts? "I don'ts knows whats plurals Maxes means," I admitted.

"Shh," Hallie said, brushing her slim fingers through my hair. Her manicured nails felt good along my scalp. "Babies needs heads scratches."

"Everyone's havings sexes," I lamented. "'Cept Maxes."

Hallie said something to one of her brothers and within moments, pushed a bottle of water into my hands. "Chug, sweetie."

So I did. I was nothing if not obedient. When that one was empty, she handed me another glass of wine except this one was suspiciously clear and tasted a lot like water.

"Wha's dis?" I asked, studying it.

"Pinot Aqua. It's new."

"Huh." I guzzled it down even though it wasn't as tasty as the other stuff. After a while, I realized I'd been played. "I blame you for the loss of my good buzz."

Hallie lifted a perfectly waxed brow. "Then I hope you blame me for your lack of hangover tomorrow too."

"Mpfh." It only made me sober enough to really realize that everyone was getting lucky except me. "Wah," I threw in for good measure.

As we watched men toss their partners over their shoulders for whatever the precursor to the walk of shame was, the sexual tension in the room thickened like... thick... whatever.

Now I couldn't stop thinking about thick things. I wanted some thick things. I glanced over at the beautiful be-suited man standing against a far wall. Arthur radiated calm patience. I wondered idly how many times he'd had to stand around watching a bunch of people get drunk off their asses.

Asses.

I tilted my head back and forth, opening first one eye then the next to see if I could catch a glimpse of the man's posterior. He caught me gawping at him.

I groaned and accidentally blurted my thoughts out loud. "For the love of god, is there any gay man willing to toss me over his shoulder and take me to his bed?"

Arthur's eyes heated. Almost in slow motion, he stepped away from the wall and bent at the waist in a formal bow.

"Sir, allow me."

It was like something out of a movie. He strode over to me and scooped me up, proving to the entire room that age doesn't mean you can't go caveman on a dude.

"Eep," I squeaked when he tossed me over his shoulder. "Omigod, is this happening?"

He smelled like money. Not a dirty wad of crumpled up bills, but some kind of elegant, old-world fragrance that I thought must have been formulated especially for my heart. Or dick. Or something.

"Yes," I muffled into the back of his suit coat. "Yes, please."

"Your room or mine, ma crevette?"

I spoke French, but wondered if my buzzed brain was misremembering the word for necktie.

My brain spun with the options of which room we should escape to. "Um... I... huh?"

His warm hand ran up the back of my thigh to my ass like he was exploring the prize he'd won at the fair. It gave me the guts to put my own palms possessively under the tail of his jacket and feel the firm cheeks under the smooth wool of his suit. The minute I grabbed on, they flexed.

"Sweet Jesus," I moaned. "That's... that's a nice set of... muscles."

His light chuckle made me wish I could see his face, so I was glad when he got us into a room and set me down on the floor in front of him. Arthur's eyes were intense and focused directly on mine.

"Hi," he said softly. "I'm Arthur Biancheri."

My heart thump thumped. "Max Wilde."

"Will you let me take you to bed, Max Wilde?"

"Please." It came out in a scratchy croak so I cleared my throat and tried again. "I'd like that more than anything."

Arthur's hands slid into my hair on either side of my head, my eyes drifted closed, and a sigh escaped my lips. I was expecting his mouth on mine, our first kiss, but that's not what happened.

His hands moved to my collar and began opening my shirt as his lips brushed across my cheek to my ear, his breath hot along my skin.

"Je te veux," he whispered into my ear.

I want you.

"Oh god," I breathed.

"T'embrasser..."

To kiss you.

His lips brushed down my neck, the tip of his tongue coming out to taste my collarbone, and back up to my other ear.

"Te toucher," he murmured.

To touch you.

"Arthur," I whimpered. "Please."

"What do you want, ma crevette?"

"Kisses."

Arthur's lips caressed my jaw before teasing my mouth. When he finally pressed in with a full-on kiss, I tasted traces of white wine and sexy man. What a heady combination.

I sank against him as his mouth took charge of me, exploring and teasing, while his hands moved around to grasp my back and my neck to hold me close. I felt like a puddle of want and need. My dick pulsed against the front of his suit pants, but every time I tried to press my hips against him, he shifted.

I wanted to speed things along, to get him naked as soon as possible. After pushing his jacket off, I worked his tie open and began picking desperately at his buttons.

"Too fucking tiny. Help," I pleaded. "I can't... my fingers don't work."

Arthur's smile was indulgent. "Let me. Finish getting undressed and lie on the bed, beautiful."

I scrambled out of my clothes like they were on fire and I threw myself on the pristine hotel bed. Naked starfish ready and willing. All I needed was a distinguished valet to climb on and pound me into the mattress.

After sending up a particularly polite but harried prayer to the gods of lube and condoms, I glanced over at Arthur to see what the holdup was.

"Hngh," I babbled as soon as I saw him standing there in naked splendor. The man was fit and hung like a motherfucking porn star. If porn stars had pretty-pretty, giant uncut dicks. Which, they did. *"Nnnngh."*

"Acceptable?" he teased. "Not going to kick me out?"

"Gnfh," I said with the international double hand signal for *gimme that dick.*

He crawled onto the bed and dropped open mouth kisses from my ankle to my inner thigh, running his warm hands over my calves and thighs and hips until reaching for my straining cock

"Are you drunk right now, Max?" he asked, meeting my eyes.

I knew what he was asking and I wanted there to be no mistaking my consent. "I was earlier, but I'm not now. Ok, maybe a little buzzed still, but I know exactly what I'm doing, Arthur. I want this. I promise."

He nodded and smiled which only deepened the laugh lines by his eyes and made me want him more. The man was sexy as fuck.

After teasing all around the base of my cock with his mouth, he finally took it into his mouth.

"God yes," I cried when what I really wanted to do was chant *suck it, suck it, for the love of god, suck it.*

I ran my fingers into his thick hair, reveling in the few waves that had defied his styling products. I wanted to mess this pristine valet up and see him flushed and debauched from fucking me senseless.

As he bobbed over my cock, teasing the crown with his talented tongue, I threw my head back in pleasure.

And almost knocked myself out on the headboard.

3

ARTHUR

I HEARD the bang and looked up. Tears filled Max's eyes suddenly and overflowed onto his flushed cheeks. I realized he'd hurt himself on the headboard.

"Cripes," I said, crawling up his body to examine his head. "Baby, what happened?"

His beautiful dark eyes met mine. His lashes were deep black with shining droplets of tears caught in them. "Hit my head like an idiot."

"Oh, sweetheart," I murmured as I moved around to take a look at the back of his head. "I'm so sorry."

"I'm so stupid," he said with a sniff. I moved his hand out of the way and felt gingerly for a bump. Sure enough, one was forming. I moved off the bed and began to throw on some clothes. He looked at me with wet eyes. "Where are you going?"

"To get some ice. I'll be quick. Get under the covers and stay warm, alright?"

"I'm sorry," he said again. "I ruined everything."

I smiled at him and walked over to kiss his forehead before clasping his face and forcing him to look at me. "You ruined nothing. I love to take care of people. Let me do this."

He reluctantly nodded so I grabbed the key card and ice bucket before exiting the room in search of an ice machine. Once I found it, I returned and made up an ice compress with a hand towel. When I sat next to him on the bed, he automatically leaned in to my side. I moved us around until he was lying sideways on my lap and I could hold the ice on his head.

"How'd you become a valet?" Max asked. "You said you like to take care of people. Is that how you...?"

"It's actually sort of an inherited position," I explained. "My father and grandfather were also in service to the monarchy. So it was a natural thing for me to pursue."

"Do you like, intern or something for that?"

"Sort of. I was sent to boarding schools and university to get the same education as Lior. It's very different from a house servant or something like that. While many of my duties are domestic, I also help manage his life in ways people don't expect. That's why I need to have a high level of education. Because a valet is often someone a royal spends copious amounts of time with, we have quite a bit of influence on them. For that reason, there are very high standards of both education and integrity. At least, that's how it's done in our country."

"Wow. I had no idea. That's really interesting. Do you like it?"

I couldn't keep my hands out of his dark curly hair. "I do like it. Mostly because I love Lior like a brother and making his life easier makes me happy."

Max turned over to face me. He was so cute and sexy, my heart thumped faster when he looked at me.

"That's really sweet," he said. "I feel that way about my family too."

I brushed the curls back from his forehead, but they fell back as soon as my hand moved away. "What do you do for a living?"

"I'm a nanny." His cheeks pinked and his eyes cast down as if there was something to be ashamed of.

I tilted his chin up with my finger. "That's amazing. The kids must love you."

His smile was self-deprecating. "They love me because they have me wrapped around their little finger. Despite all my early childhood classes in college, I'm total mush when one of them quivers a chin at me."

"Do you want kids of your own one day?"

Max shrugged. "I don't know. Probably not. I love being able to walk away at the end of the day. Maybe that sounds terrible, but I have dreams that don't really include kids."

"Like what?" I shifted so we were lying side-by-side facing each other. After reaching for his hand, I held it in mine and toyed with his fingers.

"I want to travel. I love history and art. Felix has told me so much about Gadleigh Castle, and I want to actually see places like that, you know?"

I nodded and smiled. "It's amazing. I'd love to show it to you. I'm sure Felix would too. Why haven't you come visit before?"

He blushed and looked down again which honestly hardened my dick inappropriately. I couldn't help it—he was so sweet and delightful.

"I want someone to share it with. And I..." He shrugged. "I don't really date. I've had some bad experiences, so..." He shrugged again. "Anyway, I'll see it one day."

My heart tightened in my chest. I leaned in and kissed him softly, telling him without words that he was worthy of being taken care of.

After I'd lost my breath from kissing him, I pulled back. "Will you stay with me tonight, crevette?"

"Doesn't that mean necktie?" he asked. His eyes were glazed from the kisses and his lips were puffy.

"Cravate is necktie. Crevette is..." I eyed him, wondering if he'd take offense. "Shrimp."

Max smiled and leaned in to kiss me again, muttering something about how sexy men can make any word sound sexy. I didn't pay much attention to it because I was too busy noticing the pain from earlier wasn't in his eyes anymore. As we kissed, I wrapped my arms around him and pulled him on top of me, turning onto my back and wrapping my legs around the back of his.

He was hard, and the tip of his cock left sticky streaks across my stomach as he pressed into me. My hands cupped his glorious ass, and I realized I was a selfish bastard. How could I want to fuck him after he'd smashed his head only a little while earlier?

"I'm fine," he muttered into my mouth. The little devil could read my mind. "Please. I want you, Arthur."

I ran my hands all over him, up his slender back and across his rounded shoulders. When my grip returned to his ass cheeks, I pulled him in tight to me.

"Can I please—"

He cut me off. "Yes! Yes. Whatever you're asking, the answer is yes."

I smiled and ducked down to suck on his neck before flipping him onto his back and moving back down to his cock to resume the oral pleasure I'd been giving him before he bumped his head. Once he began gasping and begging, I couldn't hold back anymore.

I needed to be inside him.

4

———————

MAX

I'll be honest. I'm sort of slutty anyway. But being with Arthur made me absolutely brainless and desperate. I begged him to fuck me, whimpering like a sex-starved lunatic.

He sucked down my cock like a pro, but that wasn't what I wanted from him. I wanted his dick in my ass. I wanted to feel full of him, to feel joined together and be able to look in his eyes while he thrust into me.

"Please," I asked again. "Arthur."

"You're so beautiful right now, sweetheart. Flushed and wild-eyed. Just look at you," Arthur murmured as he kissed a path back up to my neck. The man knew exactly how to kiss the right spots to make me dizzy.

"Fuck me," I said, panting like an over-excited puppy. "Need you inside me. Need you, *need you.*"

"Shhh. I have you, ma crevette. Je t'ai."

I have you.

I moaned again and closed my eyes in surrender. Patience. I could do this.

While I concentrated on the feel of his soft lips, the gentle scrape of his evening whiskers, he must have somehow magicked up some lube because suddenly his fingers were at my entrance slick and demanding.

I tried to say something along the lines of *yes, please*, but it came out more of a garbled choke. Arthur's sexy rumble of a laugh warmed everything inside of me.

His fingers circled and teased until finally pressing in and working my body into compliance. I writhed beneath him and enjoyed every second of it.

When Arthur finally began pressing his fat cock into me, I gasped. My knees were folded up by my face and my hands explored every inch of his lightly furred chest.

"Keep going. So good," I told him, finally focusing enough to meet his eyes. "You feel amazing inside me, Arthur."

His face softened into a kind of tenderness. I felt like his beloved treasure when he looked at me like that. I couldn't imagine what it would be like to be his partner, the man he loved. Because even just being in bed with him for this one night was incredible and made me feel cherished and invincible.

I squeezed my eyes for a split second when the stretch became uncomfortable, and he immediately stopped.

"Breathe, sweetheart."

I reached up to cup his face. He was so sweet, so kind. "It's fine. Keep going." I wrapped my legs around him to pull him in.

When he started moving again, he leaned in to kiss me. His tongue entered my mouth right when his dick pressed past my gland and shot fireworks through my body.

"Good god, do that again," I begged. "Oh god. Arthur, fuck."

He thrust into me with increasing speed as I cried out and clutched at him.

"Tu est mon fantasme devenu réalité."

You are my fantasy come to life.

His voice barely made it into my ears, but when it did, I heard the affectionate tone and knew he had a heart. I felt both owned and cared for at the same time.

"*Arthur*," I cried as he pegged my gland again. My cock was rock hard and leaking all over my stomach. As soon as I cried out his name, he reached for me and began stroking me off in time with his thrusts. It felt so fucking good.

"Ah fuck. *Fuck.*" I gasped and came in warm shots all over his hand and my own stomach. The shocks of pleasure throughout my body stole my breath, but when I finally sucked in some air, I heard Arthur grunt before calling my name.

After his climax, Arthur locked eyes with me, pinning me with his intense stare. We were both still gasping for breath, but it seemed like something was shifting between us. It hadn't felt like an anonymous quick fuck to me.

I'd gone into this hoping to get laid. But now... now I wanted to stay the night with him, to curl up against his sexy, strong body and sleep in the protection of his arms.

I drew an index finger along his jaw. "You... that... I don't know what to say."

Please don't make me go.

Arthur continued to study me for a beat before speaking. "I have not had enough of you, ma crevette. You will need to stay with me until I have."

But he never did.

So when Felix and Lio announced admitted the following morning they wanted to have kids sooner rather than later and made a joke about hiring me as their nanny, it didn't seem like such a joke. It seemed like fate.

Which is how I ended up staying with Arthur forever.

PROFESSOR PLATONIC

1

———————

JACK

I STARED at my email while the blood drained from my face to my toes.

To: Jack Wilde

We regret to inform you your application for participation on the Raintree Arctic Ecology and Evolution research expedition was not successful.

There was more to it than that. Probably. Bullshit explanations about how many qualified candidates had applied and how tough the competition had been. How hard it was selecting only one recipient for the honor.

And I understood it all. Of course I did. Graduate students from around the world had applied to go on the groundbreaking expedition. They couldn't take everyone.

But I was devastated. Not getting the research fellowship meant having to go home to Dallas and listen to my mother complain about my "denial of real-life responsibilities" and my father ask me yet again when I was going to "stop fussing with that environmental nonsense and get a real job."

"You look like you're gonna hurl, dude," my cousin Hallie said before popping a potato chip in her mouth. She was visiting Houston for the weekend to see a friend's art show and had stopped by my apartment to drop off a suit my mom had bought me. An interview suit. "What's up?"

"I didn't get a spot on the research expedition this summer," I said, feeling numb. "Everyone I talked to said they thought I was already considered part of the team. My application was supposed to be a formality."

She settled into the hand-me-down sofa my roommate had left behind when he'd moved out. If I didn't find another roommate soon, I was going to have to give up the lease and find a cheaper room to rent next semester. It was either that or ask my parents for help, which would occur precisely when hell froze over.

"What do you think happened?" Hallie asked. "I thought you were already working with the people leading the expedition?"

"I was. I *am*." Not only had I helped craft the grant proposal that was funding the expedition, but I'd also helped originate some of the research planned for the expedition. I was one of Dr. Raintree's favorite grad students.

It didn't make any sense.

The only person who hadn't seemed all that convinced had been my evolutionary biology professor.

My stomach dropped. *Professor Henry*. The only person in my academic community who still treated me with cold indifference had been responsible for one of the two most important recommendations on my application.

If I hadn't been chosen for the expedition, it had to have been something Professor Henry wrote.

My fingernails bit into my palms. "That fucking bastard," I hissed under my breath.

Hallie's eyes widened. "Who?"

"My evolutionary biology professor. He was supposed to write me a recommendation for the program, but the man hates me. He won't even make eye contact with me and acts like every time I ask him a question, I'm wasting his time. I'm sure this is on him."

"Why would he hate you? You're smart as hell and the hardest worker in the whole family."

I loved my cousin's loyalty. She was a fierce defender of the people she loved. I shot her a smile. "Thanks, Hallie. But it doesn't matter. It's done. I can't argue with their decision without doing further damage to my reputation. And these are the researchers and professors who can hopefully help me get a job after I finish my degree, not to mention some of them will be on my thesis committee. I'm sure it'll be fine. I just..." I sighed.

I was so fucking tired. I'd worked my ass off lately, holding down a full-time job as a lab technician while also pursuing a graduate degree. Because Barrington University wasn't cheap, I'd worked hard to try and get my degree completed as quickly as I could so I would rack up the least amount of debt possible.

In case my parents were right and I couldn't make a go of this as a career.

I shrugged. "I was already feeling sorry for myself after taking my evolutionary biology final this morning. Even though I thought I did well, the professor's probably going to screw me on the grade."

"Okay," Hallie said, rolling the chip bag closed with a loud crinkle and sitting up. "You know what you need? Hug therapy."

My family was a little strange.

"You sound like your hippie sister-in-law," I muttered. One of my Wilde cousins had married a woman named Nectarine who did yoga and believed in all kinds of woo-woo shit.

"I read an article about this last week, and I'm dying for someone to try it. Remember when you and I were at Doc and Grandpa's anniversary trip and everyone was all, 'Oh, gee, look at my soul mate who wants to sex me up and then spoon me adorably all night,' and you and I were like, 'Ew, how about just the spoon part?'"

I stared at her, trying to figure out what the hell she was trying to say. I did recall having said that, but I'd been lying through my teeth. I'd wanted the sex too; I'd just wanted the comfort more.

She sighed. "So the article I read mentioned there's an app that's like a dating app but also has other things like a classified section for getting help doing stuff around the house and whatever. Shit like that."

"You mean Heart2Heart?"

She pointed at me. "Yes, that's it. Well, they have this platonic section where you can seriously just say you want someone to hold hands or spoon with. This article talked about... wait. *Dude.* I sent you the article! You didn't read it?"

She didn't wait for me to answer before waving her hand in the air like it didn't matter. "Anyway, I sent it to you because it was about the evolutionary need for human touch and how it's become a biologic imperative for... I don't know. Some brainiac bullshit about neural circuitry. The point is. You need some."

I blinked at her. "I need some."

I needed some all right, but I needed the kind of human touch with a dick involved. And hard fucking. I needed angry sex to work out my frustration over this expedition rejection. That was what I *wanted*, at least. But I wasn't going to pursue it.

I was taking a break from sex with strangers after a particularly bad experience with a guy who was too annoying and rough. The experience hadn't turned dangerous, but it had been just close enough to remind me it *could* have. And I didn't need that kind of stress right now on top of everything else.

"It would be nice to have someone to snuggle with," I admitted. "I can't think of the last person I slept with where there was spooning involved."

Hallie sighed. "Yeah. Same. You haven't really dated anyone since Lowell, have you?"

I glared at her. "I've just been rejected from the most important career opportunity of my life, and you have to bring up Lowell? Do you hate me?"

She stretched her leg across the sofa to nudge my hip with her foot. "Sorry, Jack. He was an ass. Probably still is. Besides, he probably wasn't any good at cuddling to begin with. The man was about as comforting as a bag of sticks and rocks."

Hallie wasn't wrong. My ex was not only stiff and oddly formal, but he was also all elbows and knees. And way more interested in marine microplastics and their effect on food webs than me. Which was fine. Ocean pollutants were, indeed, a serious issue. But so was my need for affection.

"Great, now I've slipped from disappointed to morose," I muttered. "Maybe I need alcohol."

Hallie leaned forward and grabbed my laptop. "No. You need a big bear of a guy to snuggle the shit out of you tonight. I'm going to hook you up."

I ignored her as she began typing because my mind was suddenly diverted by the mention of a big bear of a guy.

Professor Henry was a big bear of a guy. I'd spent the first two weeks of my first semester daydreaming about him naked. Unlike many of my previous science professors, Professor Henry was fairly young. I'd have been surprised if he was even close to forty yet.

He was tall and broad, thick with muscles, and broody as fuck. His thick, wavy hair always seemed to be windblown and matched the dark beard he wore. Which, of course, perfected the lumberjack look he had to have been going for with his typical "jeans and flannel shirt" ensemble.

But he was a hateful asshole. Obviously. After those first two weeks of ignorant bliss, I'd learned he had it out for me. He called on everyone except for me. He returned my assignments with harsh notes of criticisms and warnings to do better.

And he'd even avoided me during his office hours.

That had stung like a bitch.

I'd run into Yi Shao coming out of Professor Henry's office, beaming as if she'd been privy to the answers for the upcoming exam. But when I'd knocked on the doorframe to ask him a quick question, he'd gruffly explained he was already late for a departmental meeting and would have to answer my question via email instead.

His answer had been short and unhelpful. He'd reminded me

that the most successful graduate students were the ones who knew how to seek the answers they needed without expecting them to be handed to them on a silver platter.

Professor Henry's admonishment had intimidated me and caused me to second-guess my relationship with every other professor in the program.

And now here I was, facing another rejection at his hands.

I felt my confidence crumbling. Normally, I had a positive outlook and was pretty good at overcoming challenges like this, but tonight... tonight I really was tempted to crawl into the comforting arms of a stranger and accept whatever affectionate touch I could get.

I glanced up to see Hallie's eyebrows lifted in question and her fingers poised on the keyboard. *Will you let me do this for you?*

I blew out a breath and nodded.

Why the hell not? One night in a stranger's arms for platonic snuggling. If I didn't stop to think about how pathetic it sounded, it might turn out to be a nice change from the alcohol-induced pity party I'd already planned.

After a semester of feeling like I was the most unlikable human on earth—thanks in part to Professor Henry—I could use a night where someone at least pretended to care about me.

2

RIVER

I STARED at the message from my mother.

Mom: *Therapeutic touch. I've decided you need some. Check out this link your father found.*

While I contemplated whether or not to entertain another one of her zany ideas, a kid in line behind me at the grocery store bumped into me, and my thumb slipped. The child's mom apologized, but I waved her off. When I looked back at my phone, the link had loaded.

My sister would say that was fate telling me to look at the link. My brother would say that was nothing but an obnoxious kid fucking with my life.

Since I was an academic who craved information of all kinds, I couldn't help but read the information on the screen.

I've had a very bad day and could really use a hug. Male ISO male for platonic but affectionate sleepover. No sex or commitments. I don't want to talk about it, just hold me all night and tell me it's going to be okay.

Something about the listing made my heart squeeze. I had uncomfortably similar feelings. And the guy who'd posted it sounded so melancholy, I wanted to do exactly as he'd said and pull him into my arms to tell him everything would be okay.

But since I was also a realist who'd heard way too many horror stories of dating apps gone awry, I was for sure not going to pursue it.

I also knew better than to engage with my mom about this, so I ignored her message and paid for my groceries before hopping in my Jeep to head home. Even though I had a handful of undergrad exams left to grade, I had a four-day weekend to get them done. After the disappointing workweek I'd had, I was in desperate need of at least one night off from the demands of my job.

My phone rang halfway home, and I sighed. I considered ignoring her call, but then guilt took over.

"Hi, Mom," I said instead.

"I just feel so awful about what's happening in your department." Typical Mom. No segue. She just dove right in and cut to the heart of the matter with a knife.

"It's not my department anymore," I corrected. "Today was my last day."

"No, I know. And you can be sure your father and I will be thrilled to have you closer to home, but I still can't believe that professor has the nerve to keep working there after the scandal he caused."

"Thankfully, no one knows about it yet," I reminded her. I didn't want to think about the drama in my department at work. I was grateful I'd been recruited away from Barrington before the scandal had come to light, and I especially looked forward to moving back to the Northeast. Texas had never been my favorite place to live, and I missed my family and friends.

Mom's voice had a dreamy quality. "My son... a Yale professor." She sighed, and I could hear the smile in her voice. "Just imagine the bragging I can do at bridge night."

I barked out a laugh as I pulled into the driveway of my rental house. "Bridge night" was the name she and her colleagues used when they got together once a month to discuss civil engineering's intersection with architecture. Telling her fellow Cornell professors that her son was taking a position at Yale was like waving a red flag in front of a particularly snotty—albeit incredibly well-educated—bull.

"Go for it. Now that the semester is over, I give you permission to brag as much as you want. Thanks for keeping it quiet up to now. I didn't want to jinx anything."

"I understand. Now all that's left is to pack up your stuff and start the long drive."

She made it sound so easy, but she probably also assumed that I didn't have four years of crap accumulated everywhere, including my lab at work. The idea of having to go through it all in the next two weeks was exhausting.

… just hold me all night and tell me it's going to be okay.

The guy who'd posted on that app had voiced my own feelings. Part of me wanted nothing more than to curl up with someone tonight and hide from my obligations and the work ahead. But I wasn't sure I was capable of holding someone all night without wanting to kiss them and touch them sexually.

Could I do it?

"River, honey?"

I snapped back to the conversation with my mom. "Yeah." I turned off the ignition and grabbed my phone and messenger bag. "Sorry. I just got home."

"Well then, I'll let you go. But I just wanted to say congratulations. We're very proud of you."

I heard my dad's voice in the background but couldn't make out what he was saying.

Mom laughed. "Dad says if you're too close-minded—by which he means boring and repressed—to consider therapeutic touch, you could always get a massage. I'm sure there are plenty of places in Houston. Just don't go to one of those 'happily ever after' ones."

I snorted. "I think you mean 'happy ending,' and don't worry." I didn't tell her that the app she'd sent me also offered plenty of "happy endings" for free. I didn't need to pay to have someone stroke me off.

After finishing the call and unlocking the back door, I went about my usual routine of watering my houseplants, checking the mail, and spending way too long reading over a flier for commemorative gold coins.

Which was when I realized that, holy shit, I actually *was* boring and repressed.

And I *still* couldn't get that Heart2Heart post out of my mind.

I didn't want someone to stroke me off. What I wanted was for someone to give a shit about me. Reassure me that I wasn't making a big mistake by leaving my current research project and my students to move across the country to a university where tenure wouldn't be guaranteed.

I pulled up the post again and stared at it.

I've had a very bad day and could really use a hug.

This nameless, faceless stranger had managed to put my feelings into words. And he had the balls to ask for help which was something my father, as a psychologist, had worked very hard to instill in me.

My thumb hovered over the Reply button.

And then I clicked it.

3

JACK

My hands were shaking. I wondered idly if I was more nervous about the expense of a hotel room than about meeting up with a stranger, but I had to admit it was most likely the hotel room thing.

I'd hooked up with strangers from an app before, so that wasn't quite as nerve-racking. But then again, it was always a little worrisome when I hadn't seen a photo of the guy to make sure he wasn't a fellow student. Or worse, a professor.

My stomach flipped over. What were the chances it would be one of my professors? Zero. Completely zero chance. First of all, two of my professors were women. Second, one of them was pushing retirement age and seemed happily married to his wife of a million years.

Thirdly, the only other professor remaining in the list of possibilities was Professor Henry. And he was definitely not the kind of guy who would respond to a post on an app. He was sure as hell not someone who would respond to a request for *comfort*.

I felt myself relax. The thought of Professor Henry offering a student a hug was laughable. I wasn't sure his body even relaxed enough for a hug, and I sure as hell knew his demeanor was about as friendly and comforting as a crocodile having a very bad day.

I bit back a laugh imagining how Professor Henry would react to seeing me on the other side of the door. When the stranger had responded to my post, he'd written, "I've had a bad day, too, and didn't know how much I needed a hug until I saw your post."

That was definitely not written by any of my science professors. But if it had been, Professor Henry would take one look at me, sniff judgmentally, and turn on his heel without a word.

Asshole.

Just thinking of him made my blood boil. The more I thought about it, the clearer it became that he'd had it out for me all semester. I had to remind myself there were kind people out there in the world who supported students. People like Dr. Malley, who'd contacted me from Royce University to inquire about whether or not I'd consider a transfer to help work on her research on the evolution of infectious diseases in the local black-capped chickadee population. Or Professor Jin from Dalhousie, who'd emailed me about an expedition in Nova Scotia the following semester that still had room for another research student.

After getting the rejection from Raintree, I realized I needed to take some time to consider where I wanted to go next. Maybe I didn't want to stay here at Barrington if Professor Henry was going to be such an obstacle to my academic success.

The firm knock on the door made me jump. At least I didn't need to think about my academic career right now. Right now, I only needed to accept a hug and physical affection from a random stranger.

I took a deep breath and opened the door.

When my brain inadvertently put Professor Henry's face on the poor stranger from Heart2Heart, I blinked rapidly to try and clear it away.

It didn't work.

"Mr. Wilde," he said in his familiar deep voice. The voice that reached down into my belly and made me want to *crawl*.

I couldn't breathe. This wasn't right. This couldn't be happening. I blinked several times more, silently begging my brain to fix this horrifying malfunction.

When I tried sucking in a breath, I made a wheezing sound and knew without a shadow of a doubt I was suffocating.

"Sorry," I gasped, letting go of the door to move back into the room. *Air.* I needed air. I wasn't getting any air. Maybe the window...

"What's...? Fuck... Jack? Jack!" His firm grip around my elbow startled me and caused my toe to catch on the carpet. I pitched sideways, but Professor Henry's arms came around me to keep me from falling face-first onto the bed.

I couldn't catch my breath, and the fear I was actually going to suffocate made it exponentially worse. Still, part of me still felt like this had to be a dream because I couldn't conceive of a world where Professor Henry *called me by my first name.*

"Can't... br... br..."

He moved me to the foot of the bed and sat me down before squatting down between my knees and taking my face in his big, warm hands. "Look at me."

I blinked again. *Please let this be a horrible mistake. Please tell me this isn't happening.* Just when I thought I'd reached the lowest possible level of mortification, I learned I had further to fall.

"Jack," he barked. "Listen to me right now, and do as I say. You are okay. It's okay. Look right here at the space between my eyes. See this? There's a little freckly spot right there. My sister says it's the shape of a tennis racquet."

I couldn't help but do what he asked. His voice had always been deep and in charge. When he spoke, people listened, and it was no different with me.

I focused on the tennis racquet.

"Breathe slowly," he said, lowering his voice and slowing it down. My eyes widened in surprise at the gentle tone, but I was too panicked to say anything.

His thumbs brushed over my cheekbones. "Shhh. Slow it down... that's it... in... out... You're okay. You're okay."

I felt hot tears of embarrassment fill my eyes and spill over before I could blink them away. "S-s-sorry," I whispered, still trying to breathe. "Y-you d-don't h-have..."

"Shhh. Don't try to talk. I'm here. I'm not going anywhere." He hesitated for a minute before flashing me an easy smile, something I'd never, ever seen on his face before. It was like the sun coming out from behind a dark rain cloud.

The damned thing lit up the entire room and made my heart throw itself against my ribs.

"Besides," he continued. "If I'm not mistaken, you owe me a hug."

I squeezed my eyes closed in mortification and felt more tears spill out. This was the absolute worst moment of my life.

And it was happening in front of Professor Henry.

How would I ever recover from this?

4

RIVER

When the door opened, revealing Jack Wilde on the other side, my heart had done a funny little dance of confusion. First, I couldn't help but think how incredibly inappropriate it would be for me to engage in any physical touch with a student, but then I'd reminded myself he was no longer my student.

I'd already turned in all of my grades for graduate students. The only remaining grades outstanding were for a few students in a low-level undergraduate course.

After I'd successfully reminded myself the fraternization rule didn't apply here, I felt indescribably giddy.

I was going to get to hold Jack Wilde in my arms all night long.

If he would let me.

This was too good to be true. I'd had an inappropriate crush on this particular grad student since three days before the semester started when I'd seen him jogging on a treadmill at the gym while trying to hold back a bad case of the giggles at something on his phone.

He hadn't succeeded.

I'd watched him nearly stumble off the equipment while snorting with laughter. Every time he'd tried to get control of himself, he'd look back at the phone and start laughing again.

He was magnetic. I couldn't keep my eyes off him. Even now, I wanted to drink in every facet of his beautiful face.

But he was panicking. And I couldn't blame him.

I'd spent the entire semester terrified of stepping out of line, of being caught staring, or worse, getting hard in front of the damned class because he was just that sexy.

His eyes were bright blue green, and his sandy-brown hair was slightly overgrown and always looked messy, like he'd rolled out of bed after being well fucked all night. He was quick to smile and even quicker to make a new friend and put others at ease.

He was the holy trifecta of funny, sweet, and smart.

I wanted him more than I'd ever wanted anyone, including the celebrity crushes I'd had as a preteen.

But Jack Wilde was off-limits.

Or he had been. Now he simply hated me.

I'd done everything I could to avoid him. It had been neither professional nor pretty. I'd avoided eye contact in class. I'd resisted calling on him for fear I would be seen playing favorites. And I'd written the shitty recommendation that had cost him his dream placement on the Raintree expedition.

No wonder the very sight of me had made him choke.

I moved up onto the bed next to him and put my arm around him, pulling him into my chest. How did I explain all of this? How did I even begin to apologize?

His voice was muffled at first until I realized I was holding him too tightly. "What?" I asked.

"I was trying to focus on the tennis racquet."

"I'm sorry," I said, meaning it more genuinely than anything I'd ever said to another human being. "I... I need to explain."

Jack's breathing was finally slowing down, and the fact he could make a complete sentence was a very good sign.

"It's fine," he said. "I'm feeling better anyway."

He tried to pull out of my embrace, but I tightened my arms without thinking. "Don't."

Jack lifted his face to me. His eyes were red-rimmed but still bright and beautiful. The tip of his nose was pink from being pressed against my shirt. "I'm okay," he said again. As if that was the only reason I was holding him.

"I'm not," I admitted softly.

Jack studied me for a minute before snuggling into my chest again and returning the hug. We stayed like that for a long time, holding each other without a word of explanation or understanding.

Except... except I did understand. I understood why he needed this. Why he needed comfort.

One of his professors had screwed him over by denying him a spot on the research expedition he'd so desperately wanted.

I pulled away from him and moved to squat in front of him again so I could see his face. He looked surprised and confused but didn't say anything. I wondered if he was scared or hurt or angry.

Without thinking, I took both of his hands in mine, which only seemed to make his shock more intense. His eyes were almost comically wide.

"I need to tell you something," I said, scraping my teeth over my lip. "And I couldn't tell you before now because I was your professor, and also the university was trying hard to keep it under wraps."

Jack blinked, his inky lashes still wet from tears. "What... what is it?"

"It's about your research," I began.

Jack's nostrils widened, and his lips pursed. "Oh."

"No, wait," I said quickly, trying to think. *Just spit it out, asshole.* "It's not what you think."

"Really? Because I think you fucked me over by sabotaging my application."

He could see the truth on my face because he yanked his hands out of mine.

"Jack," I said. "I did. But let me explain."

He pushed me until I rocked back on my heels and hit the ground on my ass. Clearly, he wanted to get away from me. Instead of following him over to the large window, I rested against the dresser and waited.

"Go on," he said after a minute. He didn't turn to face me. Instead, he looked out the window as if the Houston skyline had something interesting to offer.

"Raintree is part of a fraudulent research grant scheme."

He turned to face me. His expression was fiercely defiant. "What? No way."

I balled my hands into fists to keep from going over there to hold him again. I wanted to touch him so fucking badly. Instead, I focused on giving him the explanation he deserved.

"It's true. Dr. Raintree has been pocketing the bulk of the grant money. He gets his grad students to help apply for research grants, the grant money comes to him, and then he half-asses the research and pockets most of the money. He's had two expeditions in the past five years get canceled for bad weather, and the money hasn't been returned or used for other research."

Jack stared at me in disbelief as his brain worked through what I was saying. He was a smart guy. I knew he'd have done his research on the Raintree expeditions, and he'd know about the canceled trips.

"How do you know about this?" he asked.

I sighed and dropped my chin to my chest. "I've been watching him for the past four years. I finally couldn't stand it anymore, and I said something to the dean. If... no, *when* word gets out, it's going to put all of us in a bad light. The university wanted time to mitigate the fallout."

"You turned him in?" he asked.

I nodded cautiously. I couldn't decide if he thought I was a terrible human being for ratting out a colleague or a decent one for trying to protect the students and the program.

He reached up to run his fingers through his hair and yank on the ends. I could tell the information was taking time to process. "So... what does this mean for the department? Is Dr. Raintree leaving? And what about the students in the middle of research?"

"I don't know. That'll be up to the dean."

My fingers itched to touch him. Now that I was here, now that I knew he wanted—no, *needed*—touch, I couldn't stop imagining my hands on him.

"Come here," I said.

Jack's eyes widened. "W-why?"

"I want to hold you."

My heart thundered even though I tried my best to project a calm, controlled demeanor.

"Why?" he asked in a slightly higher-pitched voice.

Instead of answering him, I pinned him with a look—one I hoped held all the longing and frustration I'd been repressing for an entire semester.

Jack's chest rose and fell before he whispered, "You can't mean it."

"I do. I wanted to hold someone tonight. It's been a hell of a week. A hell of a *semester*. My colleagues turned their backs on me when they learned what I'd done. I had to find another job. I felt so isolated and alone, I was willing to take comfort with a stranger. But now that I know *you* were the one who wrote that post... I want it even more."

Emotion flashed through his eyes. Surprise, and if I wasn't mistaken, heat. My chest tightened.

"Please," I added softly.

5

JACK

THIS WAS TOO good to be true.

I moved toward him slowly, waiting for him to laugh and admit it was all a setup of some kind. But then I saw the sincerity in his eyes. His chest heaved up and down, revealing maybe he wasn't quite as calm and collected as he appeared to be about this.

"Isn't this fraternization?" I asked weakly.

"I already turned in your grade. I'm no longer your professor."

It was true. I'd checked my grades before heading to the hotel and hadn't really been surprised at the strong showing in my evolutionary biology class. In being a total hard-ass to me all semester, it turned out Dr. Henry had managed to thoroughly prepare me for the final.

I'd aced it.

And now my hard-ass professor was summoning me to... his lap? For hugs? What was happening right now?

"I thought you hated me," I blurted.

His eyes darkened, which made my skin prickle. "That's the opposite of how I feel about you, Jack."

When he said my name, my stomach swooped and left me light-headed. It was amazing how much longing and *want* he could pack into that single syllable.

"W-why?" I hated how unsure and vulnerable I sounded right then, but I *felt* unsure and vulnerable. I'd never been good at hiding my true feelings.

Professor Henry sighed and looked down at the hands he held clasped in his lap. "Because you're beautiful and smart. You're funny and warm." He looked up at me. "You're exactly the kind of man I've always dreamed about being with."

My breathing sped up again, enough to make me wonder if another panic attack would come on. "You're messing with me," I said, stopping in my tracks before getting too close.

"Does it look like I'm messing with you?" His eyes stayed on mine with an intensity that filled the room, and I had to shake my head.

"I don't want to pressure you or do anything you don't want. So tell me... do you want me to leave?"

No. Definitely not. No. No, please.

"I don't know," I admitted, lying through my teeth.

His body language stayed relaxed, but his expression didn't. It was almost like he wanted me to listen, to understand.

"I saw you before the semester started," he said, surprising me. "You were at the gym, laughing at something on your phone. I couldn't stop staring at you."

My heart ticked wildly in my neck. I didn't know what to say, so I stayed quiet.

"You were sexy as fuck. Sweating from your run and wearing these little running shorts that revealed your long, muscled legs and your tight ass. I almost got hard right there in the student fitness center."

I hoped to God my breathing didn't sound as erratic as it felt.

He continued. "But it was your laugh that really got me. You couldn't stop. And your joy lit up the space around you. Everyone who heard you got a smile on their face. That night when I went home, I decided that if I saw you again, I was going to ask you to spend the afternoon with me... or the evening... or, fuck, forever, if you'd have let me. But you never came back to the gym—"

"I tripped over one of those electric scooters people leave all over campus," I whispered. "Tweaked my ankle."

"When I saw you walk into my classroom a few days later, my heart leapt out of my chest. There you were, *finally*, only..."

"Only, I was your student," I finished for him.

He nodded. "And I was your professor."

The puzzle pieces clicked together. His avoidance of me, the lack of eye contact, his short answers to my questions. It made sense, or... it would have, if not for the fact he was way out of my league.

"*Fuck*. But that wasn't fair," I said, feeling anger bubble up. "You should have said something. I thought you hated me. I thought I couldn't do anything right. I thought... I thought I wasn't cut out for this field!"

Professor Henry surged to his feet, grabbing me by the shoulders and leaning down to meet my eyes. "You *are*," he said with a clenched jaw. "You're one of the brightest students in the entire program, and if I made you doubt that for a single second, I'm even sorrier than I can express."

Hearing him apologize lifted a heavy burden I didn't realize I'd been carrying. I respected him as a scholar, and his approval carried weight with me. If he believed I had something to contribute to the study of evolutionary biology, then maybe I could stop second-guessing myself all the time.

Maybe I could stop listening to my parents' opinions.

"Professor—"

"I'm *not* your professor anymore," he growled. "Call me River."

River. Even thinking of him that way felt incredibly intimate.

Perfectly intimate.

"River," I said slowly, testing the syllables.

He exhaled softly.

"I wish you'd told me."

"About Raintree or about my attraction to you?"

There was the slightest hint of a smile at the corner of his mouth, and I wanted to explore it with the tip of my tongue. I was nearly giddy with the idea that I might actually get to.

I swallowed. "Both?"

"And what would you have done if I'd told you?" He moved his hands down my arms until he could weave our fingers together. My breathing hitched.

"Uh…" I couldn't think with him this close, with saliva filling my mouth and blood filling my dick.

River's eyes flicked between mine as if trying to read me. One of us moved closer.

I breathed in, catching the scent of him. Aftershave that smelled fresh and masculine. I wanted to press my nose to his neck and get more of it.

"I don't know," I admitted.

"I couldn't tell you about Raintree. All I could do was try and make sure you weren't one of the students he left hanging in the wind. I was under a legal agreement not to disclose anything—" He sucked in a breath. "You're driving me crazy," he added under his breath.

I leaned forward until my forehead was on his collarbone. He'd come here to give me comfort, so I was going to take it.

"Why didn't you tell me you wanted me?" I asked his shirt.

His arms came around me and pulled me closer. I exhaled and felt my entire body give in and relax against him.

"I didn't want you to drop the class," he admitted, nuzzling his cheek against my head. "Seeing you was the brightest spot in my week, and I couldn't give it up."

I tilted my head up until my nose brushed the skin of his neck. God, he smelled so fucking good. "I wanted you too," I admitted before letting my lips brush his neck too.

"Jack," he breathed. "I came here—" His voice cracked. "I came here to give you platonic comfort."

I reached up to grab the sides of his face with my hands and meet his eyes with mine.

"I don't want comfort anymore."

6

——————

RIVER

Jack was in my arms, hot and willing, sending me every signal he wanted me as much as I wanted him. How was this possible?

"Are you sure?" I croaked. My vaunted self-control was practically nonexistent.

Without saying anything, Jack lunged up on his toes and kissed me hard on the lips. I grabbed the back of his head to hold him there as I took advantage of the situation.

His mouth was perfect, soft and warm, open and eager. He kissed like he'd been as starved for it as I was. Even though he was shorter and smaller than me, his body was solid and strong. His physical confidence made me grin against his mouth. Now that he knew how I felt about him, he seemed much less timid.

Braver. *Determined*.

I pulled myself away from him long enough to meet his eyes. "Wait, stop," I said, setting him away from me. "I promised it would be platonic. If we're changing the rules, I need you to be sure..."

His grin was adorable and teasing. "Did I seem unsure to you when I had my tongue down your throat?" His lips were red and full, slick from our kisses, as if I'd needed visual proof.

I brushed his hair back from his face and pressed a small kiss to the apple of his cheek. "You're so fucking sexy. I can't believe you're here with me."

"Me?" he squeaked. "You're, like, Barrington's most desirable professor. Why in the world would you settle for an ecology geek like me when you could have anyone you wanted?"

"I'm an ecology geek who finds other ecology geeks incredibly attractive." I moved my mouth closer to his ear and lowered my voice. "And you forget I've seen you in your running shorts."

Jack shuddered and let out a little breathy sound. I continued teasing his face and neck with small kisses while I told him just how sexy I found him. While I spoke, his ears turned red, and his breathing sped up. He was responsive as hell, which turned me on even more and made me handsier than ever.

"Want to touch you everywhere," I admitted. My voice sounded husky and rough, which matched the animalistic feelings I was having toward him. It was getting harder and harder to hold back when part of me wanted to push him down on the bed and fuck him. *Hard*.

"Please," he breathed. "Please touch me. Want your hands—" He sucked in another shaky breath. "Everywhere."

I pulled off his shirt before dropping to my knees. When I looked up to check his expression—to make sure he was still okay with what I was doing—he looked at me with dazed eyes, a stubble-reddened chin, and glossy lips.

"Fuck, you're sexy," I said. "You're killing me. Let me suck you off."

Jack's mouth was slightly open, but all he did was nod. I reached for the button of his jeans and flicked it open before yanking down the zipper and reaching inside the dark red cotton to pull out his hard cock. It was fucking perfect. Hard and smooth with a deep pink head.

I leaned over to taste it, running the flat of my tongue down the front of his shaft before pulling the tip into my mouth and sucking.

"Oh fuck," he cried, reaching for my hair with his hands. He grasped my head and held it as if he was afraid I was going to pull off.

I wasn't going anywhere.

I bobbed my head up and down slowly, wrapping my tongue around him while I worked his pants and underwear down to his ankles.

My cock throbbed, and my balls felt heavy. Having Jack's dick in my mouth and his scent in my nose was an unexpected gift. I'd come here hoping to find a kind stranger to share a nice hug with, and now I was miraculously having sex with the man I'd been crushing on for months.

When I met his eyes again, my heart jumped. He was so fucking beautiful and sexy.

I pulled off to ask him what I could do to make him feel good. His grin was adorable. "Uh, that was feeling pretty damned good, to be honest. More of that would be—*gnffff*!"

I swallowed him down and reached for his sac, rolling his nuts in my hand and pressing a finger behind them. Jack's fingers tightened in my hair as he let out the most amazing sounds. I wanted more of them. I wanted to see him come completely unraveled because of me.

My mouth stayed on his hard, wet cock while I did my best to remove his clothes. Jack mumbled incoherent things, which made me smile around his shaft. He was so fucking sweet, I wanted to take care of him. To hold him. For more than just one night.

I couldn't believe my luck, that I was here with him like this.

His body was gorgeous. Lithe and fit, healthy and strong. He smelled like soap, and I realized he was the kind of guy who would have made sure to shower out of consideration for whoever was coming to be with him tonight.

Thank *fuck* that was me.

I pulled off him and met his eyes. "Get on the bed, sweetheart."

Jack's eyes widened at the unexpected endearment, but he did as I said. I watched his bare ass as he crawled across the large bed to lie on the pillows.

I waited for him to meet my eyes again, and then I took my time undressing.

7

JACK

IF I DIED RIGHT HERE and now, I could honestly say I'd lived a full and complete life.

Watching Professor Henry... *River*... take his clothes off for me was some kind of glitch in the space-time matrix that I was not going to squander.

Even if all I ever got of him was this one night, I was going to enjoy the ever-loving fuck out of it.

His shoulders were wide, and his chest was covered in dark hair. A slight layer of padding covered his abs, and it was bisected by a dark trail leading from his chest to his groin.

I wanted to lick his happy trail.

He was every fantasy I'd ever jacked off to. Big, broad, masculine. In charge.

When he pulled off his pants, the bulge in his boxer briefs revealed more than I expected and everything I'd ever fantasized about. My ass clenched in anticipation.

"Fucking hell," I said without realizing I'd spoken out loud.

River's lips widened in a grin. "Yeah? Like what you see?"

I bit my bottom lip and nodded. "I'm going to kill my cousin for suggesting a platonic sleepover. This is so much fucking better."

The sound of his deep laughter filled the room and made the last remnants of my nerves fall away. River Henry was here, he was willing, and he wanted me. Badly.

It was all I needed.

I reached down to stroke myself. "You're taking too long."

His eyes darkened. "What do you want, Jack?"

"I want you to fuck me," I admitted breathlessly. "And I want to feel your hands and mouth all over me."

He stalked toward me, his eyes so intense I felt dizzy from being their target. "You have no idea how many times I've fantasized about being inside you," he said in a low growl.

My breath came faster. "Please."

Instead of joining me at the top of the bed, where I was sprawled in a puddle on the pillows, he started at the bottom. And licked his way up the inside of one of my legs.

The sound of my desperate panting filled the room. "Please," I said again. There was no other feeling left. Want. Desperate hope. "Please," I whimpered again.

He nosed my balls before licking my shaft again. When his hands grasped the back of my knees and bent them up, I clenched again.

And then his tongue landed on my hole.

My vision whited out. His mouth was aggressive and possessive. His tongue, lips, and teeth—and that fucking *beard*—owned my ass while I lay there babbling nonsense and clutching the sheets in my fists.

"F-fucking f-fuck me," I begged at one point, and his face reappeared in my vision. His hair was wildly messy, and his lips were red and wet.

"I want you so much I'm afraid I'm going to come before getting inside you," he admitted. "Condom?"

"Hm? Hm? Whuh?" It took me a minute to understand what he was asking. I shook my head frantically. "On PrEP. You?"

He nodded. "Same. You good bare? You sure?"

I nodded too and felt my heart thunder even harder. Professor River Henry was going to bareback me. I was going to feel his bare cock inside me. It wasn't something I'd done with anyone else, despite being on PrEP. Lowell had been a stickler for tidiness and hygiene, and I'd never fully trusted hookups enough to try it.

But I trusted River. And I wanted this too badly to stop.

"Lube," I gasped. "I have some in my backpack."

Before I finished saying the words, River was across the room, rifling through my bag.

"Toiletry kit," I said, reaching down to stroke my aching cock. "I was worried I might get too turned on and have to rub one out in private," I added with a breathy laugh.

River came back over with a knowing smirk. "And did you? Did you get so turned on by your platonic stranger you couldn't keep from getting hard around him?"

His thick dick bobbed heavily in front of him, and I couldn't look away.

"I'm not the only one."

"No. You're definitely not." He crawled on the bed again and kissed the tip of my dick before moving up to kiss the center of my chest and then my mouth. His heavy weight pressed me into the mattress and gave me a taste of what it would feel like to be held down by his larger, stronger body.

I had to bite back another plea.

Soon, I'd forgotten everything but River Henry and his commanding kiss. When his knee nudged my legs apart and his slick fingers began working my hole, I sucked in a breath and almost choked.

The deep rumble of his laugh vibrated through his chest into mine, and it made everything inside of me melt into a puddle of want.

River Henry owned me. And he could keep me as long as he wanted. I was his. I would do anything to feel his fat fingers teasing my hole and his rough chest hair abrading my tender nipples. To see the heat in his eyes and hear him say my name.

"Breathe," he murmured as he moved between my legs and pressed his tip against my entrance. "Push out... that's it... breathe... good... *oh god*. Fuck. Jack, *fuck*."

His dick was enormous. My ass burned in the stretch, but when he finally bottomed out, I panted through it, comforted and encouraged by a constant stream of words spoken hot against my neck.

I groaned as the pain turned into hesitant pleasure, and I suddenly realized how fucking good it was going to be. With every pulse of his hips, his cockhead brushed against my gland and lit me up inside.

I arched my head back and groaned again, which seemed to rile him up.

River's teeth grazed my neck, and I felt the bulge of his biceps behind my legs as he held them bent to the sides. When he began to move faster, in and out, I cried out and begged him to go harder, faster, *more*.

His own noises of pleasure filled the room, filled my stomach, filled my heart, as he made my body his. He took all of me, filling me up and making me want as much of him as he'd give me.

"River!" I screamed as I felt my climax barreling down. I didn't want it to end, but I wanted to feel this, feel complete release in his arms and underneath him.

"That's it. Come for me. Show me how much you want this. I'll be right there with you, Jack. Fucking hell. Your body. I can't…"

The release hit me full force, contracting my muscles and sending my brain flying. I was only vaguely aware of River shouting my name, his hot, damp skin against mine, the thick, delicious burn of his cock inside me, and the scent of our spunk between us.

It was the single hottest moment of my life.

8

RIVER

I wanted to laugh. I wanted to sing. I wanted to shout my incredulity from the rooftops.

Jack Wilde lay a sweaty heap underneath me. His stomach was coated in jizz, and he had a goofy grin on his face. It shouldn't have been life-changing... but I knew it was. The single night that would change the course of my life forever.

I was going to fall in love with this man.

I knew it the way I'd known I was gay the summer I turned fourteen and saw a Nike ad on television. I knew it the way I'd known that I was meant to study biology. It was simply one of the truths of my life.

"Why are you staring at me like that?" Jack asked, suddenly looking self-conscious.

"I want more than this," I blurted with no finesse whatsoever.

His eyes flashed with pain and disappointment. He tried to roll away from me as my words hit my ears, and I realized how they'd sounded.

"Stop," I said. "I mean, wait. Stop. Please listen."

I could see Jack turtling up. He was going into insecure self-preservation mode, the same kind of emotion that had undoubtedly caused his panic attack earlier.

I brushed the sweaty hair back from his face. "Jack... I want more *with you*. I want you. But I want... I want more than one night. I want this to be the beginning of something."

The change that came over his face was breathtaking. "Really?"

I leaned in and pressed a kiss to the edge of his mouth before moving it to his cheek, his eyelid, his temple, and his forehead. "I've wanted you for a long time. I never knew you'd be interested in me too. And I..."

For some reason, my brain chose this moment to remind me of all the obstacles. I was moving back east. He was a Texas boy through and through. He—

Jack grabbed my face and forced me to meet his eyes. "Now you listen," he said. "I want that too. So whatever just made your face fall... you need to tell me right now. If you've changed your mind that fast, I need to know."

He was adorable in his newfound confidence. I wanted to see more of it.

"I didn't change my mind. But I'm moving to Connecticut. To take a job at Yale."

His face lit up. "You got a teaching position at Yale? That's incredible!"

I realized we had a lot to talk about, and I hadn't even cleaned him up yet. I rolled off him and pulled him up, throwing him over my shoulder to carry him to the shower.

He yelped and then laughed—the same pure, joyful laughter I'd heard that first day at the gym. The best sound ever.

Once I stood him up under the hot spray and joined him in a full-body hug, I exhaled.

This was everything I'd ever wanted. Comfort. Excitement. *Home.*

"I want you in every way," I admitted softly against his ear.

He pulled back and met my eye. He looked a little unsure again. "Dr. Malley who contacted me from Royce University to inquire about whether or not I'd consider a transfer to join her research team. Isn't that close to Yale?" He bit his lip. I could tell he was worried I was going to scoff at the implication of him moving with me.

But I felt the opposite. My heart soared. I leaned closer and held him extra tight. My throat felt like there was a giant knot in it. "That would be incredible," I managed to say. "Would you... would you consider it? The program there is well respected. More even than Barrington's. So even if you changed your mind about... about me..."

Jack pinched my ass, shocking me into a yelp. I pulled back and stared at him in surprise.

"I know this is fast," Jack said. "But I am ready for a change. I need to get some distance from my parents and from Texas. And if the Dr. Raintree scandal is going to break, the department here is going to take time to recover."

"So you'll come?"

"I mean... I'll need to find a roommate and an affordable place to live..." He flashed me a cheeky smile. "Know anyone in the area who might also be looking for a place?"

I grabbed him up and spun him around, kissing the hell out of him and eventually running soapy hands all over his body.

After drying each other off, we moved back to the bed and slid under the covers, talking nonstop about how much we'd hidden from each other all semester, how we'd each had secret crushes on each other, and how we planned to tackle a big move together while being careful to respect each other's boundaries.

"Okay, but..." Jack grinned at me. "I'm not sure I want to have *that* many boundaries with you."

"Same," I said with a laugh. "But I want to make sure you're happy. Always."

He snuggled closer and wrapped his arms and legs around me until we were tangled together in a delicious ball. After a few minutes, his sleepy voice made its way to my ears.

"Okay, but we can't ever tell anyone how we really met. It's way too embarrassing."

I pressed a kiss to his hair and bit back a laugh. "Not even my parents? The proponents of healing touch?"

He shook his head, releasing a faint smell of hotel shampoo into the air. "No. Because if they know, then my family will find out and tease us forever. The Wilde clan does not let things go."

Two weeks later, I realized he was right when I met most of his extended Wilde family, the gorgeous pack of cousins and their equally beautiful husbands. I was shocked by the sheer number of gay men in the Wilde family. But not at all surprised that Jack Wilde was the sweetest and sexiest of them all.

And he'd been right. As soon as they found out how we met, they never did let us live it down.

But two months later, I became one of those Wilde husbands when we spontaneously decided to get married during a trip to Las Vegas with some of his cousins. I'd never forget the moment Jack Wilde became Jack Henry.

And two years later, when I checked the mail, watered the plants, and dropped a kiss on my husband's forehead, I realized it was a damn good thing that Wildes never let anything go.

To: Dr. Jack Henry and Dr. River Henry

   We are pleased to inform you your application for sponsorship of the Henry Arctic Ecology and Evolution research expedition has been approved.

I let out a whoop that had my husband running down the hall.
"You did it, Dr. Henry," I said proudly.
"*We* did it," he replied.
And we spent the rest of the night practicing touch therapy... in a decidedly nonplatonic manner.

THE ADVENTURE CONTINUES! Check out the <u>Aster Valley series</u> for more humor, heart, and heat. What happens when an NFL coach's son falls for

his father's star player? Click <u>here:</u> https://readerlinks.com/l/1599372 to learn more about Right as Raine.

WILDE FAMILY LIST

Grandpa (Weston) and **Doc (William "Liam")** Wilde (meet in *Wilde Love*)

Their children (oldest to youngest):
Bill, married to **Shelby**
Gina, married to **Carmen**
Brenda, married to **Hollis**
Jacqueline

Bill and **Shelby**

Their children (oldest to youngest):
Hudson (meets **Charlie** in *Hudson's Luck*)
West (meets **Nico** in *Facing West*)
MJ
Saint (meets **Augie** in *His Saint*)
Otto (reunites with **Walker** in *Wilde Fire*)
King (meets **Falcon** in *King Me*)
Hallie
Winnie

Cal (meets **Worth** in *NautiCal*)
Sassy

Gina and **Carmen**
↓
Quinn (meets **Beck** in *Made Marian Shorts)*
Max (meets **Arthur** in *Arthur and Max)*
Jason

Brenda and **Hollis**
↓
Kathryn-Anne (Katie)
William-Weston (Web)
Jackson-Wyatt (Jack) (meets **River** in *Professor Platonic)*

Jacqueline
↓
Felix (meets **Lio** in *Felix and the Prince)*

Non-Wildes
↓
Ignatius Corbridge and **Jon Banks** (from *The Billionaire's Valet*)
Stevie Devore and **Evan Paige** (from *Flirt*)
Miller Hobbs and **Darius Grant** (meet in *Forever Wilde in Aster Valley*)

Get to know the Wilde family and friends in the <u>Forever Wilde series</u> here:
http://readerlinks.com/l/1444583

ABOUT LUCY LENNOX

Lucy Lennox is the USA Today bestselling author of over fifty gay romance titles including the GoodReads Hall of Fame winner Wilde Love. Born and raised in the southeast USA, she is finally putting good use to that English Lit degree she earned before the turn of the century.

Lucy enjoys naps, pizza, and procrastinating. She stays up way too late each night reading romance because it's simply the best.

For more information and to stay updated about future releases, sales and audio news and to grab some free and bonus reads, please sign up for Lucy's author newsletter on her website at LucyLennox.com or to stay in the know, join her exciting reader group, Lucy's Lair on Facebook.

facebook.com/lucylennoxmm

instagram.com/lucylennoxmm

amazon.com/Lucy-Lennox/e/B01N0I0YPT

bookbub.com/authors/lucy-lennox

pinterest.com/lucy_lennox

ALSO BY LUCY LENNOX

Join <u>Lucy's Lair</u>

Get Lucy's <u>New Release Alerts</u>

Like Lucy on <u>Facebook</u>

Follow Lucy on <u>BookBub</u>

Follow Lucy on <u>Amazon</u>

Follow Lucy on <u>Instagram</u>

Follow Lucy on <u>Pinterest</u>

Other books by Lucy:

<u>Made Marian Series</u>

<u>Forever Wilde Series</u>

<u>Aster Valley Series</u>

<u>Virgin Flyer</u>

<u>Say You'll Be Nine</u>

<u>Hostile Takeover</u>

<u>Prince of Lies</u>

<u>Mister Majestic</u>

<u>Twist of Fate Series</u> with Sloane Kennedy

<u>After Oscar Series</u> with Molly Maddox

<u>Licking Thicket Series</u> with May Archer

<u>Champion Security</u> series with May Archer

<u>Honeybridge</u> series with May Archer

Visit Lucy's website at www.LucyLennox.com for a comprehensive list of titles, audio samples, freebies, suggested reading order, and more!